高级英语
读写译
教　程

孙书兰　翁建秋　蔡旭东 编著

 东南大学出版社
·南京·

内 容 简 介

　　《高级英语读写译教程》是研究生英语系列教材之一,是继学完大学英语教学大纲规定内容后的提高阶段教材。此教程的编写充分考虑了非英语专业硕士研究生的实际水平。书中课文主要选自国外近年书刊,题材广泛,经典耐读,内容涉及现代科学技术、社会文化等方面,具有较强的知识性和趣味性。全书包括 12 个单元,每单元有两篇阅读文章,分别配以形式多样的练习,有利于学生复习巩固语言知识,训练提高语言运用技能。

　　本书适用于各类非英语专业硕士研究生使用,也可供具有中等以上英语水平的读者自学进修使用。

图书在版编目(CIP)数据

高级英语读写译教程 / 孙书兰等编著. — 南京 ：东南
大学出版社,2011.8
研究生英语系列教材
ISBN 978 - 7 - 5641 - 2929 - 3

Ⅰ. ①高… Ⅱ. ①孙… Ⅲ. ①英语—阅读教学—研究
生—教材②英语—写作—研究生—教材③英语—翻译—研
究生—教材 Ⅳ. ①H31

中国版本图书馆 CIP 数据核字(2011)第 166631 号

高级英语读写译教程

编　　著	孙书兰　翁建秋　蔡旭东				
责任编辑	李　玉		封面设计	王　玥	
责任印制	张文礼				
出版发行	东南大学出版社				
出 版 人	江建中				
社　　址	南京市四牌楼 2 号		邮　　编	210096	
经　　销	全国各地新华书店				
印　　刷	溧阳市晨明印刷有限公司				
开　　本	787mm×1092mm　1/16				
印　　张	8.75				
字　　数	228 千字				
版　　次	2011 年 8 月第 1 版　2011 年 8 月第 1 次印刷				
书　　号	ISBN 978 - 7 - 5641 - 2929 - 3				
印　　数	1—5000 册				
定　　价	28.00 元				

(凡因印装质量问题,可直接向读者服务部调换。电话:025—83792328)

高级英语读写译教程

出版说明

　　《高级英语读写译教程》由东南大学外国语学院研究生英语教研室组织编写,是研究生英语系列教材之一。此教程的编写充分考虑了非英语专业硕士研究生的实际水平,适合各类非英语专业硕士研究生以及具有中等以上英语水平的读者自学进修使用。本系列教材还包括《高级英语视听说教程》。

　　本教程的编写目的在于进一步扩大和巩固学生的常用词汇和语法基础知识,增强学生的阅读理解能力,训练和培养学生的写译能力以及一定的口头表述能力,使学生运用英语的各项技能得到进一步的提高,以满足日益增长的国际交流与合作的需要。

　　本教程中所选课文题材广泛,内容丰富,主要涉及现代科学技术、社会文化等方面,经典耐读。文章大多选自国外近年来的书刊,有较强的知识性、科学性和趣味性。学生可以不囿于自己专业的狭小天地,广泛涉猎各种读物,在扩大知识面、增加对文化背景了解的过程中,达到对英语的习得。

　　本教程的练习部分突出了对学生运用语言能力的培养。每单元有两篇分别适合于精读和泛读的文章,每篇文章后分别配以阅读理解、词汇、完型填空或改错、写作和中英互译等语言技能的运用练习。练习形式多样,单项和综合练习兼而有之,并吸收了全国研究生英语入学统一考试、大学英语六级考试、TOEFL、SAT 等测试题型的长处。

　　全书共有 12 个单元,由孙书兰负责选材组稿。第 1、3、6、7、11、12 单元的 Section A 部分由翁建秋编写,第 2、4、5、8、9、10 单元的 Section A 部分由蔡旭东编写,12 个单元中的 Section B 部分由孙书兰编写。

　　本教程在编写过程中得到了东南大学外国语学院和东南大学出版社的鼎力支持和热情关怀,在教材编写过程中提出了宝贵建议,在此一并表示诚挚的谢意。

　　尽管我们在本书的编写中尽了最大的努力,但恐难以做到尽如人意。由于水平有限,加之时间紧迫,错误和疏漏之处在所难免,热忱欢迎各位同行和广大读者朋友在本书的使用过程中给我们提出宝贵意见并加以指正。

编　者

2011.8

目 录

Unit  1

Section A   Intensive Reading and Writing

The Green Banana

By Donald Batchelder

[1] Although it might have happened anywhere, my encounter with the green banana started on a steep mountain road in the interior of Brazil[1]. My ancient jeep was straining up through spectacular countryside when the radiator began to leak, ten miles from the nearest mechanic. The over-heated engine forced me to stop at the next village, which consisted of a small store and a scattering of houses. People gathered to look. Three fine streams of hot water spouted from holes in the jacket of the radiator. "That's easy to fix," a man said. He sent a boy running for some green bananas. He patted me on the shoulder, assuring me everything would work out. "Green bananas," he smiled. Everyone agreed.

[2] We exchanged pleasantries while I mulled over the ramifications of the green banana. Asking questions would betray my ignorance, so I remarked on the beauty of the terrain. Huge rock formations, like Sugar Loaf[2] in Rio[3], rose up all around us. "Do you see that tall one right over there?" asked my benefactor, pointing to a particular tall, slender pinnacle of dark rock. "That rock marks the center of the world."

[3] I looked to see if he was teasing me, but his face was serious. He in turn inspected me carefully to be sure I grasped the significance of his statement. The occasion demanded some show of recognition on my part. "The center of the world?" I repeated, trying to convey interest if not complete acceptance. He nodded. "The absolute center. Everyone around here knows it."

[4] At that moment the boy returned with my green bananas. The man sliced one in half and pressed the cut end against the radiator jacket. The banana melted into a glue against the hot metal,

plugging the leaks instantly. Everyone laughed at my astonishment. They refilled my radiator and gave me extra bananas to take along. An hour later, after one more application of green banana, my radiator and I reached our destination. The local mechanic smiled. "Who taught you about the green banana?" I named the village. "Did they show you the rock marking the center of the world?" he asked. I assured him they had. "My grandfather came from there," he said. "The exact center. Everyone around here has always known about it."

[5] As a product of American higher education, I had never paid the slightest attention to the green banana, except to regard it as a fruit whose time had not yet come. Suddenly on that mountain road, its time and my need had converged. But as I reflected on it further, I realized that the green banana had been there all along. Its time reached back to the very origins of the banana. The people in that village had known about it for years. My own time had come in relation to it. This chance encounter showed me the special genius of those people, and the special potential of the green banana. I had been wondering for some time about those episodes of clarity which educators like to call "learning moments", and knew I had just experienced two of them at once.

[6] The importance of the rock marking the center of the world took a while to filter through, I had initially doubted their claim, knowing for a fact that the center was located somewhere on New England[4]. After all, my grandfather had come from there. But gradually I realized they had a valid belief, a universal concept, and I agreed with them. We tend to define the center as that special place where we are known, where we know others, where things mean much to us, and where we ourselves have both identity and meaning: family, school, town and local region.

[7] The lesson which gradually filtered through was the simple concept that every place has special meanings for the people in it; every place represents the center of the world. The number of such centers is incalculable, and no one student or traveler can experience all of them, but once a conscious breakthrough to a second center is made, a life-long perspective and collection can begin.

[8] The cultures of the world are full of unexpected green bananas with special value and meaning. They have been there for ages, ripening slowly, perhaps waiting patiently for people to come along to encounter them. In fact, a green banana is waiting for all of us who leave our own centers of the world in order to experience other places.

Notes to the Text

1. **Brazil**—a country of eastern South America. The largest country in the continent, it was ruled by Portugal from 1500 to 1822 and was an empire until 1889, when a republic was established. Brasília has been the capital since 1960; São Paulo is the largest city. Population, 119,002,706. 巴西,首都是巴西利亚,最大城市是圣保罗。

2. **Sugar Loaf**—i. e. Sugar Loaf Mountain, a granite mountain at the entrance to the harbor of Rio de Janeiro.

3. **Rio**—i. e. Rio de Janeiro, a city of southeast Brazil on Guanabara Bay, an arm of the Atlantic Ocean. According to tradition, it was first visited in January 1502 by Portuguese explorers who believed Guanabara Bay to be the mouth of a river and therefore named the city Rio de Janeiro

(River of January). It became capital of the colony of Brazil in 1763, of the Brazilian empire in 1822, and of the independent country in 1889. In 1960 the capital was transferred to Brasília. Population, 5,090,700. 里约热内卢(巴西港市，州名)

4. **New England**—a region in the northeastern corner of the United States consisting of the six states of Maine, New Hampshire, Vermont, Massachusetts, Rhode Island, and Connecticut. New England is bordered by the Atlantic Ocean, Canada (the Canadian Maritimes and Quebec) and the State of New York.

Part I Comprehension of the Text

1. Why did the villagers gather to look when the author was forced to stop on the mountain road?
2. What is "a learning moment"? What are the two learning moments the author experienced?
3. Why did it take a while for the author to understand the significance of the rock marking the center of the world?
4. What did the author think of the green banana before and after the encounter with it?
5. What lesson did the author draw from his experience?

Part II Vocabulary

A. Choose the one from the four choices that best defines the underlined word or phrase.

1. As later Stone Age people migrated out of Africa, they <u>encountered</u> new environments with different climates or plants and animals.

   A. removed from   B. confined by   C. exposed to   D. met with

2. A long, screaming run was capped with a <u>spectacular</u> jump that threw sparkling sheets of water into the air!

   A. breathtaking   B. eye-catching   C. everlasting   D. far-reaching

3. Other animals sometimes have, or seem to have, conflicting desires, but we alone are able to <u>reflect</u> on the possible consequences of different actions.

   A. predict   B. consider   C. diminish   D. eliminate

4. In exchange, Edward would commit to serving his <u>benefactor</u> in whatever ways he should need assistance for life.

   A. superior   B. advisor   C. helper   D. savior

5. He doubted if her fair skin had ever glimpsed the sun or her <u>slender</u> fingers performed hard labor.

   A. slim   B. flexible   C. delicate   D. swift

6. Some of the boys <u>teased</u> him about his lack of athletic ability when he attempted to play games on the playground.

   A. made a play for   B. made a fuss over   C. made fun of   D. made mention of

7. The message he sought to <u>convey</u> to his readers was that they should remove their prejudice toward people of different religions.

   A. show off   B. get over   C. carry through   D. put across

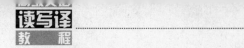

8. We all expected that the horse was killed, but to our underline{astonishment}, when the load was taken off him, he arose to his feet and appeared to be but little injured.

    A. great surprise   B. great delight   C. great anger   D. great fear

9. Scientists in Hawaii have made a underline{breakthrough} in developing a stronger disease-resistant pearl oyster.

    A. complete failure   B. sudden appearance   C. vital discovery   ·   D. total destruction

10. Finally we used a particular specification of the model to discuss a number of policy issues from the underline{perspective} of developing countries.

    A. supposition   B. viewpoint   C. expectation   D. direction

B. Choose the one from the four choices that best completes the sentence.

1. A good balanced meal would _____ of some lean protein, some vegetable or fruit portions and maybe a starch.

    A. assist   B. consist   C. insist   D. resist

2. The teacher, with dispassionate authority, _____ the boy on the head and sent him back to his place.

    A. struck   B. beat   C. patted   D. slapped

3. Nothing further was known about the incident, but the captain _____ the passengers that the crew would be conducting a thorough investigation.

    A. assured   B. insured   C. assumed   D. ensured

4. The importance of _____ design becomes evident when we realize how much time we spend surrounded by four walls.

    A. internal   B. external   C. interior   D. exterior

5. Some of the members demanded to know why they had been kept in _____ of the true facts until they reached the present critical stage.

    A. connection   B. opposition   C. preparation   D. ignorance

6. All good ideas start somewhere and need a goal in order for them to flourish and reach their _____.

    A. destitution   B. desperation   C. destination   D. designation

7. The parallel sides of streets, the parallel tracks of a railroad, and the parallel tops and bottoms of walls all seem to _____ as they recede into the distance.

    A. converse   B. submerge   C. disperse   D. converge

8. The legacy of Persian history and the enduring popularity of its art have _____ to every corner of the globe.

    A. filtered through   B. broken through   C. carried through   D. got through

9. To maintain production levels, we must _____ and develop or acquire new oil and gas reserves to replace those depleted by production.

    A. search   B. examine   C. identify   D. locate

10. If things do not _____ as expected, there will be a fall in the market value and the investor may suffer a capital loss.

    A. turn out   B. work out   C. make out   D. come out

C. Complete each sentence with the proper form of the word given in the parenthesis.

1. These fires have wreaked havoc in the community, caused tremendous property damage, and caused _____ suffering. (calculate)

2. This scenario was even suspected by many scientists in the decades after Darwin's theory won _____. (accept)

3. The medal is given annually to one outstanding individual in _____ of personal and significant contribution to European science. (recognize)

4. If you follow these steps as you evaluate contractors, you will know that you have contracted with _____ and confidence. (clear)

5. The working panel of the meeting was attended by the _____ of the Danish shipping lines and journalists. (represent)

6. Consequently, our goal is to review the existing empirical literature to better assess those factors that may affect the _____ of the research. (valid)

7. Most of the crops in this field are _____ but those over the circular enclosure ditches are still growing and show up as green bands. (ripe)

8. The most spectacular ice _____ are those in alpine caves where the cave's ambient temperature stays at or below the freezing point year-round. (form)

9. The theoretical model was created showing the _____ of financial valuation methods depending on investors. (apply)

10. Endeavours within the fields of arts and humanities are also of great _____ for human well-being. (signify)

Part III Cloze

Directions: Read the passage through. Then go back and choose one suitable word or phrase for each blank in the passage.

There are a great many differences between the United States and China; at times you may not understand the actions of Americans or particular facets of the American society. When you first __1__ in the United States, you, like students from other countries, may __2__ "culture shock"—a feeling of disorientation or __3__ that often occurs when someone leaves a familiar place and moves to an unfamiliar one. This is __4__ and you should not be disturbed by it. As you become more __5__ to life in the United States and to American attitudes, uncomfortable feelings should __6__. Americans usually are willing to answer questions and explain __7__ which may be unfamiliar to you, so never __8__ to ask for assistance.

It is difficult to __9__ about characteristics of Americans as US society is __10__ of persons who come from __11__ social and cultural backgrounds, who live in varying economic situations and __12__ ways of approaching and living life differ __13__. The items mentioned below are offered __14__ to encourage you to "become American", but to help ease your __15__ to life in the United States.

1. A. reach   B. travel   C. arrive   D. get

2.	A. experience	B. exercise	C. express	D. suffer
3.	A. surprise	B. dilemma	C. discomfort	D. confusion
4.	A. common	B. normal	C. ordinary	D. universal
5.	A. accustomed	B. satisfied	C. familiar	D. interested
6.	A. disappear	B. distinguish	C. diminish	D. vanish
7.	A. environments	B. conditions	C. circumstances	D. situations
8.	A. attempt	B. hesitate	C. afraid	D. intend
9.	A. generalize	B. conclude	C. think	D. generate
10.	A. consisted	B. made	C. combined	D. composed
11.	A. several	B. enormous	C. numerous	D. much
12.	A. some	B. whose	C. their	D. the
13.	A. radically	B. slightly	C. scarcely	D. merely
14.	A. also	B. only	C. both	D. not
15.	A. reluctance	B. effort	C. adjustment	D. suffering

Part IV   Writing

Directions: Develop each of the following topics into an essay of about 200 words.

1. Travel can be an excellent complement to one's education. Do you agree? Explain.

2. What is your favorite way of traveling?

3. On Eco-travel

Section B Extensive Reading and Translation

Culture Shock

By Kalvero Oberg

[1] Culture shock might be called an occupational disease of people who have been suddenly transplanted abroad. Like most ailments, it has its own symptoms and cure.

[2] Culture shock is precipitated by the anxiety that results from losing all our familiar signs and symbols of social intercourse. Those signs or cues include the thousand and one ways in which we orient ourselves to the situation of daily life: when to shake hands and what to say when we meet people, when and how to give tips, how to make purchases, when to accept and when to refuse invitations, when to take statements seriously and when not. These cues, which may be words, gestures, facial expressions, customs, or norms, are acquired by all of us in the course of growing up and are as much a part of our culture as the language we speak or the beliefs we accept. All of us depend for our peace of mind and our efficiency on hundreds of these cues, most of which we do not carry on the level of conscious awareness.

[3] Now when an individual enters a strange culture, all or most of these familiar cues are removed. He or she is like a fish out of water. (1) <u>No matter how broad-minded or full of goodwill you may be, a series of props have been knocked from under you, followed by a feeling of frustration and anxiety.</u> People react to the frustration in much the same way. First they reject the environment which causes the discomfort. "The ways of the host country are bad because they made us feel bad." When foreigners in a strange land get together to grouse about the host country and its people, you can be sure they are suffering from culture shock. Another phase of culture shock is regression. The home environment suddenly assumes a tremendous importance. To the foreigner everything becomes irrationally glorified. All the difficulties and problems are forgotten and only the good things back home are remembered. It usually takes a trip home to bring one back to reality.

[4] Some of the symptoms of culture shock are excessive washing of the hands; excessive concern over drinking water, food dishes, and bedding; fear of physical contact with attendants; the absent-minded stare; a feeling of helplessness and a desire for dependence on long-term residents of one's own nationality; fits of anger over minor frustrations; great concern over minor pains and eruptions of the skin; and finally, that terrible longing to be back home.

[5] Individuals differ greatly in the degree in which culture shock affects them. Although not common, there are individuals who cannot live in foreign countries. However, those who have seen

people go through culture shock and on to a satisfactory adjustment can discern steps in the process. During the first few weeks most individuals are fascinated by the new. They stay in hotels and associate with nationals who speak their language and are polite and gracious to foreigners. This honeymoon stage may last from a few days or weeks to six months, depending on circumstances. (2) If one is very important, he or she will be shown the show places, will be pampered and petted, and in a press interview will speak glowingly about goodwill and international friendship.

[6] But this mentality does not normally last if the foreign visitor remains abroad and has seriously to cope with real conditions of life. It is then that the second stage begins, characterized by a hostile and aggressive attitude toward the host country. This hostility evidently grows out of the genuine difficulty which the visitor experiences in the process of adjustment. There are house troubles, transportation troubles, shopping troubles, and the fact that people in the host country are largely indifferent to all these troubles. They help, but they don't understand your great concern over these difficulties. Therefore, they must be insensitive and unsympathetic to you and your worries. The result, "I just don't like them". You become aggressive, you band together with others from your country and criticize the host country, its ways, and its people. But this criticism is not an objective appraisal. (3) Instead of trying to account for the conditions and the historical circumstances which have created them, you talk as if the difficulties you experience are more or less created by the people of the host country for your special discomfort.

[7] You take refuge in the colony of others from your country which often becomes the fountainhead of emotionally charged labels known as stereotypes. This is a peculiar kind of offensive shorthand which caricatures the host country and its people in a negative manner. The "dollar grasping American" and the "indolent Latin Americans" are samples of mild forms of stereotypes. The second stage of culture shock is in a sense a crisis in the disease. If you come out of it, you stay; if not, you leave before you reach the stage of a nervous breakdown.

[8] (4) If the visitors succeed in getting some knowledge of the language and begin to get around by themselves, they are beginning to open the way into the new cultural environment. Visitors still have difficulties but they take a "this is my problem and I have to bear it" attitude. Usually in this stage visitors take a superior attitude to people of the host country. Their sense of humor begins to exert itself. Instead of criticizing, they joke about the people and even crack jokes about their own difficulties. They are now on the way to recovery.

[9] In the fourth stage, your adjustment is about as complete as it can be. The visitor now accepts the customs of the country as just another way of living. You operate within the new surroundings without a feeling of anxiety, although there are moments of social strain. Only with a complete grasp of all the cues of social intercourse will this strain disappear. For a long time the individual will understand what the national is saying but is not always sure what the national means. (5) With a complete adjustment you not only accept the food, drinks, habits, and customs, but actually begin to enjoy them. When you go home on leave, you may even take things back with you; and if you leave for good, you generally miss the country and the people to whom you become accustomed.

Part A Translate English into Chinese

I. Translate the underlined sentences in the above text into Chinese.

II. Translate the first two paragraphs in the above text into Chinese.

Part B Translate Chinese into English

I. Translate the following sentences into English with the words or phrases in the passage in Section B.

1. 神经即将崩溃的症状之一是相信自己的工作极端重要,休假将会带来种种灾难。
2. 未来旅游业的发展将以政府投入为主,发挥市场配置资源的基础性作用,全力推进旅游基础设施和配套设施建设。
3. 约翰穿着打补丁的裤子和破旧的皮夹克,和这些衣冠楚楚的人在一起,觉得一点也不自在。
4. 每个人都可以分清好坏,可以通过同情之心培养道德之心,因为人性本善。
5. 同时,应该鼓励年轻人和他们的同龄人交往,发展他们的交际能力,这将帮助他们极大地减少对父母的依赖并且保持健康的精神状态。

II. Translate the following paragraph into English.

　　我能想象的惟一的希望就是:我们都同意去信仰我们所希望的,去崇拜我们所选择的,但是我们要承认每一个人都和我们一样是人,都值得受到同样的尊敬和关爱。在生物学、生理学和心理学方面,人类是完全一样的:我们都需要爱、和平、安全、食物、衣服和住所;我们都必须睡眠、繁衍后代,我们做这一切的方式一样,结果也一样。在镜中,你可以看到我,我可以看到你,但我们所接受的文化却以它们独特的方式告诉我们要注意我们在肤色、语言、服饰、饮食、婚姻、信仰等方面的不同,这使我们彼此分隔开来。

Unit 2

Section A   Intensive Reading and Writing

How to Write with Style

By Kurt Vonnegut

[1] Newspaper reporters and technical writers are trained to reveal almost nothing about themselves in their writings. This makes them freaks in the world of writers, since almost all of the other ink-stained wretches in that world reveal a lot about themselves to readers. We call these revelations, accidental and intentional, elements of style.

[2] These revelations tell us as readers what sort of person it is with whom we are spending time. Does the writer sound ignorant or informed, stupid or bright, crooked or honest, humorless or playful? And on and on.

[3] Why should you examine your writing style with the idea of improving it? Do so as a mark of respect for your readers, whatever you're writing. If you scribble your thoughts any which way, your readers will surely feel that you care nothing about them. They will mark you down as an egomaniac or a chowderhead—or, worse, they will stop reading you.

[4] The most damning revelation you can make about yourself is that you do not know what is interesting and what is not. Don't you yourself like or dislike writers mainly for what they choose to show you or make you think about? Did you ever admire an emptyheaded writer for his or her mastery of the language? No.

[5] So your own winning style must begin with ideas in your head.

1. Find a subject you care about

[6] Find a subject you care about and which you in your heart feel others should care about. It is this genuine caring, and not your games with language, which will be the most compelling and seductive element in your style.

[7] I am not urging you to write a novel, by the way—although I would not be sorry if you wrote one, provided you genuinely cared about something. A petition to the mayor about a pothole in front of your house or a love letter to the girl next door will do.

2. Do not ramble, though

[8] I won't ramble on about that.

3. Keep it simple

[9] As for your use of language: Remember that two great masters of language, William Shakespeare[1] and James Joyce[2], wrote sentences which were almost childlike when their subjects were most profound. "To be or not to be?" asks Shakespeare's Hamlet. The longest word is three letters long. Joyce, when he was frisky, could put together a sentence as intricate and as glittering as a necklace for Cleopatra[3], but my favorite sentence in his short story "Eveline" is this one: "She was tired." At that point in the story, no other words could break the heart of a reader as those three words do.

[10] Simplicity of language is not only reputable, but perhaps even sacred. The *Bible*[4] opens with a sentence well within the writing skills of a lively fourteen-year-old: "In the beginning God created the heaven and the earth."

4. Have guts to cut

[11] It may be that you, too, are capable of making necklaces for Cleopatra, so to speak. But your eloquence should be the servant of the ideas in your head. Your rule might be this: If a sentence, no matter how excellent, does not illuminate your subject in some new and useful way, scratch it out.

5. Sound like yourself

[12] The writing style which is most natural for you is bound to echo the speech you heard when a child. English was Conrad's[5] third language, and much that seems piquant in his use of English was no doubt colored by his first language, which was Polish. And lucky indeed is the writer who has grown up in Ireland, for the English spoken there is so amusing and musical. I myself grew up in Indianapolis, where common speech sounds like a band saw cutting galvanized tin, and employs a vocabulary as unornamental as a monkey wrench.

[13] In some of the more remote hollows of Appalachia[6], children still grow up hearing songs and locutions of Elizabethan times. Yes, and many Americans grow up hearing a language other than English, or an English dialect a majority of Americans cannot understand.

[14] All these varieties of speech are beautiful, just as the varieties of butterflies are beautiful. No matter what your first language, you should treasure it all your life. If it happens to not be standard English, and if it shows itself when you write standard English, the result is usually delightful, like a very pretty girl with one eye that is green and one that is blue.

[15] I myself find that I trust my own writing most, and others seem to trust it most, too, when I sound most like a person from Indianapolis, which is what I am. What alternatives do I have? The one most vehemently recommended by teachers has no doubt been pressed on you, as well: to write like cultivated Englishmen of a century or more ago.

6. Say what you mean

[16] I used to be exasperated by such teachers, but am no more. I understand now that all those antique essays and stories with which I was to compare my own work were not magnificent for their datedness or foreignness, but for saying precisely what their authors meant them to say. My

teachers wished me to write accurately, always selecting the most effective words, and relating the words to one another unambiguously, rigidly, like parts of a machine. The teachers did not want to turn me into an Englishman after all. They hoped that I would become understandable—and therefore understood. And there went my dream of doing with words what Pablo Picasso[7] did with paint or what any number of jazz idols did with music. If I broke all the rules of punctuation, had words mean whatever I wanted them to mean, and strung them together higgledy-piggledy, I would simply not be understood. So you, too, had better avoid Picasso-style or jazz-style writing, if you have something worth saying and wish to be understood.

[17] Readers want our pages to look very much like pages they have seen before. Why? This is because they themselves have a tough job to do, and they need all the help they can get from us.

7. Pity the readers

[18] They have to identify thousands of little marks on paper, and make sense of them immediately. They have to *read*, an art so difficult that most people don't really master it even after having studied it all through grade school and high school—twelve long years.

[19] So this discussion must finally acknowledge that our stylistic options as writers are neither numerous nor glamorous, since our readers are bound to be such imperfect artists. Our audience requires us to be sympathetic and patient readers, ever willing to simplify and clarify—whereas we would rather soar high above the crowd, singing like nightingales.

[20] That is the bad news. The good news is that we Americans are governed under a unique Constitution, which allows us to write whatever we please without fear of punishment. So the most meaningful aspect of our styles, which is what we choose to write about, is utterly unlimited.

8. For really detailed advice

[21] For a discussion of literary style in a narrower sense, in a more technical sense, I recommend to your attention *The Elements of Style*, by William Strunk[8], Jr. and E. B. White[9]. E. B. White is, of course, one of the most admirable literary stylists this country has so far produced. You should realize, too, that no one would care how well or badly Mr. White expressed himself, if he did not have perfectly enchanting things to say.

Notes to the Text

1. **William Shakespeare** (1564—1616)—an English poet and playwright, widely regarded as the greatest writer in the English language and the world's pre-eminent dramatist. He is often called England's national poet and the "Bard of Avon". His surviving works, including some collaborations, consist of about 38 plays, 154 sonnets, two long narrative poems, and several other poems. His plays have been translated into every major living language and are performed more often than those of any other playwright.

    "Hamlet", summit of his art, is one of Shakespeare's great tragedies. Shakespeare took an old story of murder and revenge from medieval Danish history and used it to reflect the feudal-bourgeois English society of his time and his attitude toward that society. "To be or not to be" is selected from Hamlet's Soliloquy, Act III, Scene I.

2. **James Joyce** (1882—1941)—Irish novelist and poet, whose psychological perceptions and innovative literary techniques, as demonstrated in his epic novel *Ulysses*, make him one of the most influential writers of the 20th century. Joyce was born in Dublin on February 2, 1882, the son of a poverty-stricken civil servant. As a undergraduate, Joyce published essays on literature. Joyce attained international fame with the publication (1922) of *Ulysses*, a novel, the theme of which are based on Homer's *Odyssey*. "*Ulysses*" is regarded as the most important of James Joyce's works. "*Eveline*" is one of his many short stories.

3. **Cleopatra** (69—30 B. C.)—When Cleopatra ascended the Egyptian throne, she was only seventeen. She resigned as Queen Philopator and Pharaoh between 51—30 B. C. and died at the age of 39. With the death of Cleopatra, a whole era in Egyptian history was closed.

4. **Bible**—The holy book of the Christians. It consists of the Old Testament and the New Testament.

5. **Joseph Conrad** (born **Józef Teodor Konrad Korzeniowski**; 1857—1924)—a Polish-born English novelist. Conrad is regarded as one of the greatest novelists in English, though he did not speak the language fluently until he was in his twenties (and then always with a marked Polish accent). He wrote stories and novels, predominantly with a nautical or seaboard setting, that depict trials of the human spirit by the demands of duty and honour.

6. **Appalachia**—a cultural region in the eastern United States that stretches from the Southern Tier of New York state to northern Alabama, Mississippi, and Georgia. While the Appalachian Mountains stretch from Belle Isle in Canada to Cheaha Mountain in the U. S. state of Alabama, the cultural region of Appalachia typically refers only to the central and southern portions of the range.

7. **Pablo Picasso** (1881—1973)—a Spanish painter, draughtsman, and sculptor who lived most of his life in France. He is widely known for co-founding the Cubist movement and for the wide variety of styles that he helped develop and explore. Among his most famous works are the proto-Cubist *Les Demoiselles d'Avignon* (1907) and *Guernica* (1937), a portrayal of the German bombing of Guernica during the Spanish Civil War.

8. **William Strunk, Jr.** (1869—1946)—an American writer, Professor of English at Cornell University, and author of the first editions of *The Elements of Style* (1918)—a writing guide to English usage. He privately published *The Elements of Style* for the use of his students, in the course of which it acquired "the little book" sobriquet.

9. **Elwyn Brooks White** (1899—1985)—usually known as **E. B. White**, an American writer. A long-time contributor to *The New Yorker* magazine, he also wrote many famous books for both adults and children, such as the popular *Charlotte's Web* and *Stuart Little*, and co-authored a widely used writing guide, *The Elements of Style*, popularly known by its authors' names, as "Strunk & White".

Part I Comprehension of the Text

1. What is Kurt Vonnegut arguing in his writing? What's his understanding of writing style?
2. What kind of language style does he use in this essay?
3. What does the author mean by mentioning "Picasso style and jazz style"?

4. Does the author practice what he preaches in his writing?

5. What does the author suggest at the end of this essay?

Part II Vocabulary

A. Choose the one from the four choices that best explains the underlined word or phrase.

1. He finds himself involved with a <u>crooked</u> businessman and a group of thugs who attempt to sabotage his invention.

    A. distorted   B. twisted   C. dishonest   D. deceptive

2. He remembered how proud and haughty her face was and <u>scratched out</u> the word he had written.

    A. polished   B. perished   C. deleted   D. depleted

3. If you choose credit counseling as a strategy for your debt, you must make sure you're choosing a <u>reputable</u> company and not a scammer.

    A. well-known   B. professional   C. reliable   D. respectable

4. He added that nature gave him everything he needed as a champion—unusual strength, stamina, a terrific punch, and plenty of <u>guts</u>.

    A. wisdom   B. courage   C. wealth   D. charm

5. Qualitative research strategies of interview, participant observation, and field notes were used to <u>illuminate</u> the topic.

    A. reinforce   B. decorate   C. paraphrase   D. interpret

6. He suddenly found himself <u>exasperated</u> by slow moving pedestrians, and, like a true New Yorker, began darting around them instead.

    A. provoked   B. offended   C. annoyed   D. disappointed

7. As one moves through this colourful world of Indian handicrafts, many <u>intricate</u> paintings and sculptures catch the eye.

    A. charming   B. elegant   C. delicate   D. complicated

8. Many judges will <u>acknowledge</u> that one of the most difficult aspects of a criminal case is sentencing.

    A. admit   B. assert   C. prove   D. agree

9. Its charming towns and picturesque landscapes provide the <u>enchanting</u> surroundings for your sparkling romantic holiday treat.

    A. magnificent   B. compelling   C. genuine   D. glamorous

10. Circumstances beyond my control have left me with no <u>alternative</u> but to return my vehicle to the lender.

    A. means   B. option   C. fashion   D. manner

B. Choose the one from the four choices that best completes the sentence.

1. This infinite beauty of a reverse navel ring _____ with dual colors in the trio of stones that fill the center of the continuous infinity design.

    A. twinkles   B. simmers   C. flashes   D. glitters

2. He was early _____ as a man of ability and maturity of character, a promise fully realized in his many great achievements.

    A. marked down   B. turned down   C. looked up   D. agreed upon

3. When he was not quite able to follow, Newton just took the pad from his friend's hands and _____ his own remarks into the notebook.

    A. stumbled   B. scrabbled   C. scribbled   D. scrupled

4. There are many reports of the Prophet's mastery of the Arabic tongue together with his _____ and fluency of speech.

    A. eloquence   B. sequence   C. frequency   D. delinquency

5. These stories and the principles drawn from them are _____ to you for your benefit and learning and enjoyment.

    A. commented   B. commended   C. commanded   D. commenced

6. Some applicants may _____ on about themselves in a manner that may appear self-indulgent and not very appealing to the committee.

    A. ramble   B. tumble   C. complain   D. chatter

7. Cherry tomatoes have a strong taste and are very juicy—this makes them ideal for creating this _____ sauce.

    A. vehement   B. frisky   C. disgusting   D. piquant

8. To help soldiers _____ data from drones, satellites and ground sensors, the U.S. military now issues the iPod Touch.

    A. take advantage of   B. make sense of   D. take notice of   D. make use of

9. As the same way, we need to listen to some fascinating English materials as many as possible, so that we can _____ our interest to learn it.

    A. motivate   B. cultivate   C. advocate   D. retaliate

10. Her 8-year-old daughter was adorable as she got to meet her _____, Simon, whom she praises for his negativity.

    A. image   B. idiot   C. idol   D. token

C. Complete each sentence with the proper form of the word given in the parenthesis.

1. Many philosophers hold _____ about mental properties, and many philosophers hold humility about fundamental physical properties. (reveal)

2. By the mid 20th century, humans had achieved a _____ of technology sufficient to leave the atmosphere of the Earth for the first time and explore space. (master)

3. Despite the apparent _____ of the water molecule, liquid water is one of the most mysterious substances in our world. (simple)

4. On this level, a common protocol to structure the data is used; the format of the information exchange is _____ defined. (ambiguity)

5. It was expected that these images will look charming and _____, but the final result was a bit different. (glamour)

6. I find it hard to be _____ about a man who used his wealth and power to molest children and to

then evade justice. (sympathy)

7. The question is whether or not it is possible to bottle these pheromones and use them for our own _____ advantage. (seduce)

8. Despite the gruesome images on cigarette packs, a survey shows Australian smokers are surprisingly _____ of the dangers of the habit. (ignore)

9. In several poems the reader will encounter the plain, _____ language really used by common man, and this goes straight to the heart. (ornament)

10. Many new illustrations help to _____ the text and make the book more instructive to students and practitioners. (clear)

Part III   Cloze

Directions: Read the passage through. Then go back and choose one suitable word or phrase for each blank in the passage.

It is very difficult to arrive at a full description of style that is acceptable to all scholars. As such there are many definitions of the word style __1__ there are scholars yet no __2__ is reached among them on what style is. Chapman is of the view that style is the product of a common relationship between language users. He __3__ said that style is not an ornament or virtue and is not __4__ to written language, or to literature or to any single aspect of language.

Language is human __5__ and used in society. No human language is fixed, uniform, or varying; all languages show internal variation. This variation sows the __6__ feature of individuals or a group of people which is usually referred to as style. Style is popularly __7__ to as "dress" of thought, as a person's method of __8__ his thought, feelings and emotions, as the manner of speech or writing. From the definition above, one can __9__ that style is the particular way in which an individual communicates his thought which __10__ him from others.

Style can __11__ be defined as the variation in an individual's speech which is __12__ by the situation of use. From the definition above, style is described as the variations in language usage. In __13__, style is conditioned by the manner in which an individual makes use of language.

Middleton is of the view that style refers to personal idiosyncrasy, the technique of __14__ and Chatman says that style means manner—the manner in which the form executed or the content expressed. From the definitions above, it can be deduced that style is __15__ to every individual or person and it is a product of the function of language as a means of communication.

1. A. as   B. because   C. when   D. since
2. A. conscience   B. consistence   C. conclusion   D. consensus
3. A. otherwise   B. further   C. moreover   D. besides
4. A. confined   B. confirmed   C. confronted   D. confided
5. A. friendly   B. concerned   C. specific   D. related
6. A. instinct   B. extinct   C. district   D. distinct
7. A. looked   B. referred   C. viewed   D. defined
8. A. expressing   B. explaining   C. exploring   D. exploiting

9. A. seduce   B. induce   C. deduce   D. reduce

10. A. extinguishes   B. separates   C. distributes   D. distinguishes

11. A. yet   B. also   C. either   D. only

12. A. occasioned   B. influenced   C. determined   D. demonstrated

13. A. contrast   B. return   C. addition   D. essence

14. A. exposure   B. exposition   C. disposition   D. expression

15. A. subject   B. accessible   C. unique   D. essential

Part IV Writing

Directions:Develop each of the following topics into an essay of about 200 words.

1. The Importance of Punctuation
2. The Standards of an Essay
3. Essay Writing and English Learning

Section B Extensive Reading and Translation

Variety and Style in Language

[1] All of us can change our behaviour to fit different situations. We are festive, often noisy at weddings and birthday celebrations, sympathetic at funerals, attentive at lectures, serious and respectful at religious services. Even the clothes we wear on these different occasions may vary. Our table manners are not the same at a picnic as in a restaurant or at a formal dinner party. When we speak with close friends, we are free to interrupt them and we will not be offended if they interrupt us; when we speak to employers, however, we are inclined to hear them out before saying anything ourselves. If we don't make such adjustments, we

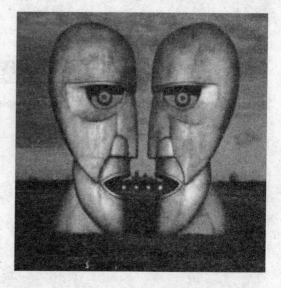

are likely to get into trouble. We may fail to accomplish our purpose and we are almost sure to be considered ill-mannered or worse. From one point of view, language is behaviour; it is part of the way we act. It builds a bridge of communication without which society could not even exist. And like every other kind of behaviour, it must be adjusted to fit different contexts or situations where it is used. When we think of all the adjustments regularly made in any one language, we speak of language variety. When we think of the adjustments any one person makes in different situations, we use the term style.

[2] Among people who are used to a writing system, there is one adjustment everyone makes. They speak one way and write another way. Most speech is in the form of ordinary conversation, where speakers can stop and repeat themselves if they sense that they are being misunderstood. They are constantly monitoring themselves as their message comes across to the listeners. But writers cannot do this. (1) They often monitor what they write, of course, going back over their writing to see that it is clear and unambiguous; but this is before the communication occurs, not while it is happening. Once writers have passed their writing on to someone else, they cannot change it.

[3] Speakers can use intonation, stress, and pauses to help make their meaning clear. A simple sentence like "John kept my pencil" may, by a shift in the stress and intonation patterns, single out through contrast whether John rather than someone else kept the pencil, whether John kept rather than just borrowed the pencil, or whether it was a pencil or a pen or something else that he kept.

[4] (2) It is true that writers have the special tools of various punctuation marks and sometimes typographical helps like capitals, italic letters, heavy type and the like; but these do not quite take

the place of the full resources of the spoken language. The sentence "Cindy only had five dollars" is not likely to be misinterpreted when spoken with light stress and no more than level pitch on "only", but in writing it could easily be taken to mean something else. To prevent ambiguity, skillful writers could change the word order to "Cindy had only five dollars" if they wanted "only" to modify "five". They would shift "only" to the beginning of the sentence if they wanted it to modify "Cindy".

[5] This simple example shows that good writers do try to avoid ambiguity. (3) As writers, they like a structure that is compact; as speakers, thinking aloud, they produce sentences that are looser, less complex, perhaps even rather jumbled. Notice, for instance, that the first sentence in the first letter to Ann Landers reads, "You have made plenty of trouble for me and I want you to know it." Like most letters to Ann Landers, this is really talk written down. The sentence contains two ideas and treats them as equals. If one is really dependent upon the other, a good writer would have written "I want you to know that you have made plenty of trouble for me." This is not to deny the effectiveness of the original sentence in this very informal letter.

[6] Speech makes more use of contracted forms. "He is" (she is) and "he has" (she has) become "he's" (she's); "cannot" becomes "can't"; "they are" becomes "they're"; "it is" becomes "'tis" or "it's"; and, with a more noticeable change, "will not" becomes "won't". So in the conversational letters to Ann Landers, contractions abound, but in the carefully prepared manuscript speeches of the Reverend Martin Luther King and President Kennedy, there are no contracted forms.

[7] Besides the difference between speech and writing there is a difference between formality and informality. A formal message is organized and well-rounded; it usually deals with a serious and important topic. Most formal language is intended to be read. Since there is no opportunity to challenge or question the writer when it is being read, the message has to be self-contained and logically ordered.

[8] At the opposite pole is the language of casual and familiar speech among friends and relatives, between people who have some kind of fellow feeling for one another. The speaker or writer is simply being him-or herself. This person knows that the others involved—rarely more than five— see and accept the speaker for what he or she is. (4) The speaker also assumes that the others know him or her well enough to make unnecessary any background information for everything that is used. The writer who signed herself "Weepers Finders" assumed that whoever read the letter would recognize the saying, "Finders keepers, losers weepers." In contrast to the formal style, this style may be called the casual style.

[9] There is also a recognizable midpoint between the formal and the casual. There are situations less rigid than the ceremonial address or the formal written message but also more structured than intimate conversation. These permit some response; there is a certain amount of give and take. Yet each speaker will feel the need to be quite clear, sometimes to explain background for the other person's benefit or in order to prevent misunderstanding or embarrassment. This middle style is known as the consultative style. It should be noted that the consultative style can allow contractions, but rarely would use slang or the incomplete expressions of the casual style.

[10] It should not be thought that speech is always informal and writing always formal. (5) The casual style is spoken more often than it is written, but it is found also in letters between friends or

family members, possibly in diaries and journals, and sometimes in newspaper columns. Formal English is typically written but may also be spoken after having first been written down. Much consultative speech is spoken, but a fair amount of writing also has the same need for full explanation even if it is otherwise quite informal.

[11] Of course, none of these styles or modes of communication is better than any other. The spoken word and the printed page are simply two different ways to communicate. Some people have thought that formal English is "the best" of the stylistic variants, but it is not. Of course, President Kennedy could not have substituted the quite casual "Nobody's here today to whoop it up for the Democrats" for "We observe today not a victory of party"; but if he had ever used the formal public speaking style at a dinner table, he would have bored everyone there. Intelligent adjustment to the situation is the real key to the effective use of language.

[12] In some respects the English language raises certain problems. In conversation some languages allow an easy distinction between the formal and the informal through their dual system of pronouns. In French, for example, intimacy on the one hand or social distance on the other are overtly marked by a choice between "tu" and "vous". English lacks such a system, but it does have a complex code of choices of title, title and surname, surname alone, given name alone and nickname, as "Doctor", "Doctor Stevens", "Stevens", "Charles", "Charley", and "Chuck".

[13] Another problem arises because of the two-layered nature of the English vocabulary. One layer consists of short, familiar words largely of native English origin (house, fire, red, green, make, talk); the other of much longer words, chiefly taken from Latin and French (residence, domicile, conflagration, scarlet, verdant, manufacture, conversation). But it is an oversimplification to equate the popular words with the casual style and the learned words with the formal style. We must admit that many Americans, especially in bureaucratic contexts, are fond of big, windy words—words that are often awkward and sometimes inexact.

[14] Although adjustment is the key to good use of the various styles, it poses problems for the student coming to English from another language. It is hard enough to become proficient in just one of the styles without having to switch from one style to another. The casual style, in particular, is not easily acquired by the nonnative speaker. Happily, this problem is not too serious. Native speakers of English are much readier to accept the features of the consultative style in a casual situation than to accept casual features in a noncasual situation. Indeed, many Americans are likely to credit a consultative speaker with greater correctness in using English than they have themselves. But even if only this one style is acquired, it is important for learners to recognize the other styles when they meet them in speech or writing and to have some sense of the situations that call for their use.

Part A   Translate English into Chinese

I. Translate the underlined sentences in the above text into Chinese.

II. Translate the first and the last paragraph in the above text into Chinese.

Part B   Translate Chinese into English

I. Translate the following sentences into English with the words or phrases in the passage in Section B.

1. 在当代英语中有许多新的语言现象,这些现象并不总是符合公认的语法规则的。

2. 他强调说他修改过的预算有很多折中的余地,并暗示议员们尽可略事更改,而不会招致再一次否决。

3. 所以我们追求幸福,将幸福与财富和成功等同起来,没有注意到拥有这一切的人不一定更幸福。

4. 与经济落后成为对比的是,贫困地区往往又是人口增长最快的地区。

5. 忽视这种差别,只看见统一方面,看不见矛盾方面,无疑是非常错误的。

II. Translate the following paragraph into English.

　　语法学家得出了他们这门科学的一些基本原则,其中三条是这个讨论的基础。第一,语言是一定社会成员所通用的一套行为模式。这是人类学家所谓的社会文化的一部分。事实上,它和文化的其他方面(如神话和礼仪)有着复杂和亲密的关系。但为了研究的目的可以作为单独的一套现象来处理,这些现象可以像其他大量的事实一样加以客观地描述和分析,特别是它的现象可以被观察、记录、分类和比较。语言行为的一般规律,可以用归纳法得出,这与用来产生物理、化学和其他科学法则的归纳法一样。

Unit 3

Section A   Intensive Reading and Writing

My Father, "Dr. Pat"

By Lindsay Patterson

A Louisiana writer remembers a "madly brilliant free spirit", the unusual and unpredictable man who was his father. How would you react to Dr. Pat if you met him?

[1] In American literature, very little has ever been written about the black middle class, particularly the Southern black middle class, which, when I was growing up, contained some of the most complex and colorful characters in American life.

[2] Among them, I believe, was my father, a madly brilliant free spirit who entered college at 16 and medical school at 18, and did not quit until he had received three medical degrees. But when I knew him he was only a dentist (a black medical doctor had already established a successful practice in our town) and a pharmacist who concocted exotic but practical remedies, his best-known remedy being Dr. Pat's Log Cabin Cough Syrup, a dark brown liquid with a sweat taste and powerful kick that was guaranteed to root out the most stubborn colds and that sold like wildfire.

[3] In addition to being a man of medicine, he was a master showman. Every Sunday afternoon he would fill the family car with cardboard cases of his Log Cabin Cough Syrup and visit four or five churches, where he was always called upon "to render a few remarks", which he began by complimenting the "sisters" on their fine appearance and the "brothers" for having the foresight and wisdom to choose such bewitching creatures. When the congregation grew still, his face grew serious, and he proclaimed in ringing tones that "Negroes should always scratch each other's backs, so we can all live on Easy Street!"

[4] The churches were mainly wood-gray structures on the edge of cotton fields beside small bleak cemeteries, and during my father's "remarks", white-uniformed ushers passed out pink and green circulars that contained his photograph, a list of his medical degrees, and an aphorism or two

("A bird in the hand is worth two in the bush"). Another circular was white and also contained his photograph and the poem "Lift Every Voice and Sing", but no mention of James Weldon Johnson as the author.

[5] In his "remarks" he recited his own poetry, as well as that of Shakespeare and Milton[1], to make the point that blacks should love and support each other, especially their professional men. To illustrate this point he would always command me and my brother to stand. "Here are my two boys", he would boom, "One is going to be a doctor and the other a lawyer. But I need your help. They're as much mine as yours, and with the Lord's help we're going to raise them right. If you ever see them doing anything wrong, you have my permission to whip their butts, and when they get home I'll whip'em some more!"

[6] The applause, the foot stomping and amens were always deafening, while my brother and I wept, for we knew that my father, who had a vile, sometimes uncontrollable temper, was as good as his word.

[7] His purpose on this earth, I was convinced, was to corrupt life. While other kids were plied with fairy tales and ghost stories, he burdened our minds with Tolstoy[2] and Shakespeare and the Bible. He screened our playmates, burned our comic books, forbade Sunday movie-going and looked upon dancing as a mortal sin, yet when my brother turned seven he decided that it was time for his firstborn to learn the "scientific facts of life". But my brother was so overwhelmed by this knowledge about "the real birds" and "the real bees", he blabbed it to everyone, including his first-grade teacher, who was so horrified that at the end of the school term she flunked him.

[8] My father was a very restless man, and it was only after his death that I learned that he had established thriving dental or medical practices in three other places before settling in our small Louisiana hometown during the late 1930's, and that in each town he had married and divorced before moving on to the next. His third wife, though, had flatly refused to dissolve their union until he had threatened to have her "put away" and declared insane.

[9] Marriage to my mother produced perhaps the happiest period in his life, but after she died he became strangely obsessed with finding a wife who held a master's degree. He eventually discovered this educational marvel in a six-foot-two haughty amazon from St. Louis, who after one month of marriage found his "two brats" a nuisance and small-town life a bore.

[10] My father, however, expressed no remorse or disappointment at her sudden departure, for he too had begun to tire of life in our town, even though he had done extremely well financially, and had built what many claimed was "the best house in town". He was also the only black man who was never called "boy", and who was invited (as a professional courtesy) to sit in White Only waiting rooms. Yet, he never was an Uncle Tom[3], which was perhaps why the "brothers" and "sisters" tried vainly to persuade him to "stay put" for the good of them all.

[11] But the promise of a new world to conquer proved, even at the age of 60, irresistible, and he set out once again to create his own extraordinary universe. Six months later, however, he was dead. Time was his only unbiased enemy.

Notes to the Text

1. **Milton** 米尔顿(1608—1674),英国诗人、政治家。代表作有三篇长诗:《失乐园》、《复乐园》和《力士参孙》。
2. **Tolstoy** 托尔斯泰(1828—1910),俄国小说家。代表作有:《安娜·卡列尼娜》、《复活》。
3. **Uncle Tom**: a black person who allows himself or herself to be treated as a subordinate to whites (from the character in Uncle Tom's Cabin, 1852, a novel by Harriet Beecher Stowe).

Part I   Comprehension Questions

1. What did the author think of his father?
2. What can be inferred about the father from what he did and said at the churches?
3. Why did the teacher flunk the author's brother at the end of the school term?
4. How many times did the father get married in his life?
5. Why did the "brothers" and "sisters" try to persuade the father not to move?

Part II   Vocabulary

A. Choose the one from the four choices that best explains the underlined word or phrase.

1. He tried to make himself the one trusted friend, to whom should be confided all the fear, the <u>remorse</u>, the agony, and so on.

   A. regret   B. sorrow   C. mortality   D. mourning

2. The glances of the young girl became milder, and she rewarded him for his decided heroism with a tender and <u>bewitching</u> smile.

   A. surprising   B. enchanting   C. exciting   D. pleasing

3. Because we want our child to do her best, we don't always notice or <u>compliment</u> her for what she does well.

   A. motivate   B. encourage   C. praise   D. convince

4. After she has a couple of drinks, she develops a <u>haughty</u> manner and walks around like she owns the place.

   A. confident   B. assuring   C. conscious   D. arrogant

5. Frustration caused by the current economic climate may lead people to take some completely <u>insane</u> actions.

   A. crazy   B. furious   C. violent   D. scary

6. We don't understand why some folks are so <u>obsessed</u> with this issue when there are so many other pressing things to worry about.

   A. fascinated   B. astonished   C. disappointed   D. dissatisfied

7. The modern world has failed to <u>root out</u> the disease because it is only treating its symptoms, instead of its causes.

A. extinguish   B. deteriorate   C. diminish   D. eliminate

8. He is employed to <u>pass out</u> the pamphlets that carry the name and contact number of the loan agent at the back.

A. distribute   B. duplicate   C. proofread   D. contribute

9. He has <u>proclaimed</u> that the path to authentic human flourishing is only found in our rediscovery of our call to communion.

A. maintained   B. announced   C. confirmed   D. established

10. He was stunned by the reaction he got: a few people suggested that he might have <u>concocted</u> the kidnapping story to buy time.

A. speculated   B. conceived   C. fabricated   D. formulated

B. Choose the one from the four choices that best completes the sentence.

1. If something can be explained simply, in a familiar way, then it is best to avoid more _____ explanations.

A. aesthetic   B. eccentric   C. ethnic   D. exotic

2. Because of the speed of the chanting he did not get all the words, so I _____ the lyrics slower while he wrote them down.

A. incited   B. memorized   C. recited   D. illustrated

3. He did what most Indians do when confronted with an embarrassing situation— _____ his head without indicating if he would comply with my suggestion.

A. scraped   B. scratched   C. scribbled   D. scrubbed

4. Effective leaders have the _____ and vision to inspire others to want to lead, the will to teach them to lead, and the faith and courage to allow them to lead.

A. foresight   B. prediction   C. prospect   D. insight

5. All ant species are unwanted in our homes because they are a _____ and frequently are found near food.

A. boredom   B. horror   C. nuisance   D. stimulus

6. Actually, naming domain names for others turned out a _____ business, especially, when you make the entire process risk free.

A. thrilling   B. striving   C. thriving   D. shrilling

7. In reflecting on his years of formal education, he is able to recall the names of all his instructors except the fifth-grade teacher who _____ him.

A. flunked   B. commended   C. complimented   D. blunted

8. Unless a person exhibits behavior that would indicate he's a danger to himself or others, the law doesn't allow you to have him _____.

A. put off   B. put out   C. put down   D. put away

9. One must never lose time in _____ regretting the past or in complaining against the changes which cause us discomfort, for change is the essence of life.

A. plainly   B. fairly   C. vainly   D. validly

10. They are now being _____ to urge their constituents to practice the tolerance and understanding which are central to the Jewish and Muslim faiths.

    A. called forth   B. called upon   C. called for   D. called up

C. Complete each sentence with the proper form of the word given in the parenthesis.

1. At some point, it occurred to some ad people that they could make ads so _____ that they would actually be passed around willingly by customers. (resist)

2. Writers who use _____ language write in ways that are free from gender and group stereotypes including race, age, ethnicity, disability or sexual orientation. (bias)

3. Hollywood actresses today are not only earning mind blowing salaries but also winning multiple awards and critical _____ from the critics. (applaud)

4. Life is so _____. You never know what will happen to you tomorrow, and where your next fortune is. (predict)

5. She avoided mention of the ongoing infighting between her and three members of the school board that led to her _____. (depart)

6. Susan, who dislikes heights, was _____ to discover that she was located on the 14th floor of a skyscraper, with two of the office walls made entirely of glass. (horror)

7. The silence of the green movement and environmentalists is _____ when it comes to urban impacts on the environment. (deaf)

8. Be _____ to all, but intimate with few, and let those few be well tried before you give them your confidence. (courtesy)

9. No one else can lessen our influence as we ourselves can lessen it through the indulgence of _____ temper. (control)

10. The pines and cypresses of hundreds years old along with the exotic flowers, rare herbs and the huge area of lawn have formed kinds of _____ spectacles. (marvel)

Part III Cloze

Directions: Read the passage through. Then go back and choose one suitable word or phrase for each blank in the passage.

    When I was growing up, I was embarrassed to be seen with my father. He was severely __1__ and very short, and when we would walk together, his hand on my arm for __2__, people would stare. I would inwardly squirm at the un-wanted __3__. If he ever noticed or was bothered, he never let on.

    It was difficult to __4__ our steps—his halting, mine impatient—and because of that, we didn't __5__ much as we went along. But as we started out, he always said, "You __6__ the pace. I will try to adjust to you".

    Our usual walk was to or from the subway, which was how he got to work. He went to work sick, and __7__ nasty weather. He almost never missed a day, and would __8__ it to the office even if others could not. A matter of pride.

    When snow or ice was on the ground, it was __9__ for him to walk, even with help. At such times my sisters or I would __10__ him through the streets of Brooklyn, NY, on a child's sleigh to the subway entrance. Once there, he would __11__ the handrail until he reached the lower steps that the warmer tunnel air kept __12__ . In Manhattan the subway station was the basement of his office building, and he would not have to go outside again until we met him in Brooklyn on his way home.

When I think of it now, I __13__ at how much courage it must have taken for a grown man to __14__ himself to such indignity and stress. And at how he did it—without bitterness or __15__ .

1. A. crumbled   B. crippled   C. crinkled   D. crimpled
2. A. balance   B. strength   C. comfort   D. courage
3. A. inquiry   B. sympathy   C. consolation   D. attention
4. A. consolidate   B. subordinate   C. coordinate   D. collaborate
5. A. think   B. say   C. act   D. hear
6. A. set   B. keep   C. take   D. hold
7. A. besides   B. during   C. except   D. despite
8. A. reach   B. make   C. bear   D. stand
9. A. impossible   B. unnecessary   C. unsuitable   D. impermissible
10. A. drive   B. push   C. pull   D. bring
11. A. resort to   B. hold on   C. conform to   D. cling to
12. A. snow-capped B. ice-free   C. dry-cleaned   D. ice-bound
13. A. marvel   B. astonish   C. puzzle   D. wonder
14. A. dedicate   B. accustom   C. subject   D. acquaint
15. A. hostility   B. disapproval   C. remorse   D. complaint

Part IV   Writing

Directions:Develop each of the following topics into an essay of about 200 words.

1. My Father or Mother
2. My Loving Sister or Brother or Cousin
3. An Unforgettable Person

Section B   Extensive Reading and Translation

This Was My Mother

By Mark Twain

[1] My mother, Jane Lampton Clemens, died in her 88th year, a mighty age for one who at 40 was so delicate of body as to be accounted a confirmed invalid destined to pass soon away. (1) But the invalid who, forgetful of self, takes a strenuous and indestructible interest in everything and everybody, as she did, and to whom a dull moment is an unknown thing, is a formidable adversary for disease.

[2] She had a heart so large that everybody's griefs and joys found welcome in it. One of her neighbors never got over the way she received the news of a local accident. (2) When he had told how a man had been thrown from his horse and killed because a calf had run in his way, my mother asked with genuine interest, "What became of the calf?" She was not indifferent to the man's death; she was interested in the calf, too.

[3] She could find something to excuse and as a rule to love in the toughest of human beings or animals—even if she had to invent it. Once we beguiled her into saying a soft word for the devil himself. We started abusing him, one conspirator after another adding his bitter word, until she walked right into the trap. She admitted that the indictment was sound, but had he been treated fairly?

[4] She never used large words, yet when her pity or indignation was stirred she was the most eloquent person I have ever heard. We had a little slave boy whom we had hired from someone there in Hannibal. He had been taken from his family in Maryland, brought halfway across the continent, and sold. All day long he was singing, whistling, yelling and laughing. The noise was maddening, and one day I lost my temper, went raging to my mother and said Sandy had been singing for an hour straight, and I couldn't stand it. Wouldn't she please shut him up? The tears came into her eyes and she said:

[5] "Poor thing, when he sings it shows me that he is not remembering, and that comforts me; but when he is still I am afraid he is thinking. He will never see his mother again; if he can sing, I must be thankful for it. If you were older you would understand, and that friendless child's noise

would make you glad. "

[6] All dumb animals had a friend in her. Hunted and disreputable cats recognized her at a glance as their refuge and champion. We once had 19 cats at one time. They were a vast burden, but they were out of luck, and that was enough. (3) She generally had a cat in her lap when she sat down, but she denied indignantly that she liked cats better than children though there was one advantage to a cat, she'd say. You could always put it down when you were tired of holding it.

[7] I was as much of a nuisance as any small boy and a neighbor asked her once, "Do you ever believe anything that boy says?"

[8] "He is the wellspring of truth", my mother replied, "but you can't bring up the whole well with only one bucket. I know his average, so he never deceives me. I discount him 90 percent for embroidery and what is left is perfect and priceless truth, without a flaw".

[9] She had a horror of snakes and bats, which I hid in pockets and sewing baskets; otherwise she was entirely fearless. One day I saw a vicious devil of a Corsican, a common terror in the town, chasing his grown daughter with a heavy rope in his hand, threatening to wear it out on her. Cautious male citizens let him pass but my mother spread her door wide to the refugee, and then, instead of closing and locking it after her, stood in it, barring the way. (4) The man swore, cursed, threatened her with his rope; but she only stood, straight and fine, and lashed him, shamed him, derided and defied him until he asked her pardon, gave her his rope and said with a blasphemous oath that she was the bravest woman he ever saw. He and she were always good friends after that. He found in her a long-felt want—somebody who was not afraid of him.

[10] One day in St. Louis she walked out into the street and surprised a burly cartman who was beating his horse over the head with the butt of a heavy whip. (5) She took the whip away from him and made such a persuasive appeal that he was tripped into saying he was to blame, and into volunteering a promise that he would never abuse a horse again.

[11] She was never too old to get up early to see the circus procession enter town. She adored parades, lectures, conventions, camp meetings, church revivals—in fact every kind of dissipation that could not be proved to have anything irreligious about it, and she never missed a funeral. She excused this preference by saying that, if she did not go to other people's funerals, they would not come to hers.

[12] She was 82 and living in Keokuk when, unaccountably, she insisted upon attending a convention of old settlers of the Mississippi Valley. All the way there, and it was some distance, she was young again with excitement and eagerness. At the hotel she asked immediately for Dr. Barrett, of St. Louis. He had left for home that morning and would not be back, she was told. She turned away, the fire all gone from her, and asked to go home. Once there she sat silent and thinking for many days, then told us that when she was 18 she had loved a young medical student with all her heart. There was a misunderstanding and he left the country, she had immediately married, to show him that she did not care. She had never seen him since and then she had read in a newspaper that he was going to attend the old settlers' convention. "Only three hours before we reached that hotel he had been there", she mourned.

[13] She had kept that pathetic burden in her heart 64 years without any of us suspecting it.

Before the year was out, her memory began to fail. She would write letters to school-mates who had been dead 40 years, and wonder why they never answered. Four years later she died.

[14] But to the last she was capable with her tongue. I had always been told that I was a sickly child who lived mainly on medicines during the first seven years of my life. The year she died I asked her about this and said:

[15] "I suppose that during all that time you were uneasy about me?"

[16] "Yes, the whole time."

[17] "Afraid I wouldn't live?"

[18] After a recollective pause—ostensibly to think out the facts—

[19] "No—afraid you would."

[20] Jane Lampton Clemens' character, striking and lovable, appears in my books as Tom Sawyer's Aunt Polly. I fitted her out with a dialect and tried to think up other improvements for her, but did not find any.

Part A   Translate English into Chinese

I. Translate the underlined sentences in the above text into Chinese.

II. Translate paragraphs 12 & 13 in the above text into Chinese.

Part B   Translate Chinese into English

I. Translate the following sentences into English with the words or phrases in the passage in Section B.

1. 任何为人父或为人母的都知道,婴儿哭闹是很正常的事,所以不要因为其他旅客的缘故而迫于压力让婴儿停止哭闹。

2. 我还得不断地想招儿,什么生日套餐啦,周末优惠卡啦,变着法儿地让他们高兴。

3. 这种看来似乎使我十分幸福的巴黎生活使我感到厌烦,因此我突然向往过那种能使我想起童年时代的安静生活。

4. 有很多美国人崇拜他,但也有几乎同样多的人认为他的魅力令人反感,令人恶心。

5. 假如由我负责的话,我就不允许游客进入野生动物保护区,那里太危险了,有许多狮子、老虎等野兽。

II. Translate the following paragraph into English.

　　我与父亲不相见已两年余了,我最不能忘记的是他的背影。那年冬天,祖母死了,父亲的差使也交卸了,正是祸不单行的日子,我从北京到徐州,打算跟着父亲奔丧回家。到徐州见着父亲,看见满院狼藉的东西,又想起祖母,不禁簌簌地流下眼泪。父亲说:"事已如此,不必难过,好在天无绝人之路!"

Unit 4

Section A Intensive Reading and Writing

The Danger of Space Junk

By Steve Olson

[1] Space may seem remote, but it's really not that far away. If you could drive your car straight up, in just a few hours you'd reach the altitude at which the space shuttle flies. The popular orbits for satellites begin twice as far up—about 400 miles above our heads. The only satellites that are truly distant from Earth are the several hundred in geosynchronous orbit, a tenth of the way to the moon. There telecommunications and weather satellites orbit at the same rate that Earth rotates, allowing them to hover above a single spot on the Equator.

[2] Since 1957 the United States and what is now the former Soviet Union have conducted about 4,000 space launches (the launches conducted by all other countries and international organizations combined account for just a few hundred additional forays into space). The leftovers from these launches—used-up satellites, the rockets that carried the satellites aloft, equipment from aborted scientific experiments—form a sort of orbital time capsule, a mausoleum of space technology.

[3] Many of the objects released into space in the lowest orbits, like Collins's camera, have fallen back to Earth. The upper atmosphere, where the space shuttle flies, gradually slows objects down; they re-enter the atmosphere and burn up within a few months or years. But a few hundred miles higher the atmosphere is so thin that it is ineffective for cleanup. Spacecraft that are launched into orbits at this height will stay in space indefinitely.

[4] Today radars that were designed to scan the horizon for incoming Russian missiles track a silent armada of space junk instead. The U. S. Space Surveillance Network[1] routinely follows more than 8,000 objects that are larger than four inches across. But Earth's orbit also contains perhaps

100,000 objects that measure from half an inch to four inches across—objects too small to see on radar but large enough to cause a spacecraft to fail. They are the land mines of space, undetected until something crosses their path.

[5] Especially troublesome are pieces of the more than a hundred rockets and satellites that have exploded in orbit. At the end of their useful lives spacecraft typically contain some fuel left over from launch or from orbital maneuvers. The fuel tanks deteriorate over time or are punctured by debris. The leftover fuels mix together and explode.

[6] It was the explosions of derelict rockets that first drew NASA's[2] attention to debris. In the 1970s Delta rockets left in orbit after delivering their payloads began blowing up. An investigation showed that the bulkheads separating the leftover fuels were probably cracking as a result of the rocket's passing in and out of sunlight. NASA began recommending that leftover fuels be burned at the end of a flight, or that they be vented into space. Since then most public and private launchers have taken similar measures—such steps are relatively inexpensive means of limiting debris. Still, every few months on average an old rocket or satellite explodes, flinging a cloud of debris into space.

[7] Eventually the number of explosions will diminish, but by then spacecraft will be breaking up for another reason. As more objects go into orbit, spacecraft will begin colliding with—and being shattered by—debris. Furthermore, collisions beget more collisions. This process is known as collisional cascading. Once it begins, the number of objects in a particular orbit will gradually increase—and the risk to satellites and manned spacecraft will rise accordingly. By the time the cascades have run their course, in a hundred years or so, even small spacecraft will suffer damaging collisions after just a few years in orbit.

[8] For many years NASA and the Department of Defense[3] were skeptical about the dangers of space debris. The problem seemed abstract, residing more in computer models than in hard experience. And it challenged the can-do mentality of space enthusiasts. Earth's orbit seemed too large and empty to pollute.

[9] To its credit, NASA has long maintained a debris-research program, staffed by top-notch scientists who have persisted in pointing out the long-term hazards of space junk even when the higher-ups at NASA haven't wanted to hear about it. Then came the *Challenger* accident[4], in 1986. NASA officials realized that their emphasis on human space flight could backfire. If people died in space, public support for the shuttle program could unravel.

[10] Engineers took a new look at the shuttle and the international Space Station[5]. Designed in the 1970s, when debris was not considered a factor, the shuttle was determined to be clearly vulnerable. After almost every mission windows on the shuttle are so badly pitted by microscopic debris that they need to be replaced. Soon NASA was flying the shuttle upside down and backward, so that its rockets, rather than the more sensitive crew compartments, would absorb the worst impacts. And engineers were adding shielding to the space station's most vulnerable areas. At this point the modules should be able to survive impacts with objects measuring up to half an inch across, and NASA is developing repair kits for plugging larger holes in the walls.

[11] But adding shielding and repair kits won't solve the real problem. The real problem is that whenever something is put into an orbit, the risk of collision for all objects in that orbit goes up.

Therefore, the only truly effective measure is a process known as deorbiting. With current technology deorbiting requires that a satellite or rocket reserve enough fuel for one last trip after its operations are finished. With enough fuel a spacecraft can promptly immolate itself in the atmosphere or fly far away from the most crowded orbits. If less fuel is available, it can aim for an orbit where atmospheric drag will eventually pull it to Earth.

[12] The logic behind deorbiting has been inescapable since the beginning of the Space Age[6], yet it has just begun to penetrate the consciousness of spacecraft designers and launchers. In 1995 NASA issued a guideline saying that satellites and the upper stages of rockets within 1,250 miles of Earth should remain in orbit for no longer than twenty-five years after the end of their functional lives. But the guideline applies only to new spacecraft and can be waived if other considerations prevail. As a result NASA and the Defense Department also continue to leave the upper stages of some of their launch vehicles in orbit, partly because existing designs do not lend themselves to deorbiting.

[13] Furthermore, the character of the Space Age is changing. The private sector now puts more payloads into orbit than do NASA and the U. S. and Russian militaries combined. A score of communications companies in the United States and other countries have announced plans that will put hundreds of satellites into orbit over the next decade. Many will fly in relatively low orbits within a few hundred miles above where the space station will orbit, so that they can relay signals coming from hand-held phones.

[14] None of these companies is under any obligation to limit orbital debris. Companies that are launching large constellations of satellites are worried about collisions between the satellites, and they are well aware that a public-relations disaster would ensue if a piece of a shattered satellite smacked the station. As a result, some plan to deorbit satellites at the end of their useful lives. But other companies are leaving their satellites up or are counting on atmospheric drag to bring them down.

[15] Government regulations covering orbital debris are still rudimentary. For now, the federal agencies that have authority over commercial launches are waiting to see if the private sector can deal with the problem on its own. But deorbiting rockets and satellites is expensive. A satellite could keep operating for several additional months if it didn't need to reserve fuel for deorbiting. Some industry representatives say they want regulations, but only if the regulations apply to everyone and cannot be evaded.

[16] International regulation will be even more difficult. Already the Russians and the Europeans launch a significant number of U. S. commercial satellites. U. S. launch companies would howl if the government imposed unilateral restrictions on spacecraft launched from U. S. territory. Extending restrictions internationally would probably require the involvement of the United Nations, which would raise a host of additional issues about the equitable use of orbits.

[17] Human societies have done plenty of things that we or our descendants may someday regret. At the beginning of the Atomic Age we seriously polluted vast tracts of land that will take many billions of dollars to clean up. We have increased the amount of carbon dioxide in the atmosphere despite a scientific consensus that global temperatures are rising as a result. We have dammed great and beautiful rivers even though the resulting reservoirs are filling with silt that will in time drastically reduce the dams' usefulness.

[18] One reason for our nonchalance is that new technologies have gotten us out of many past scrapes—and maybe they will with orbital debris, too. Perhaps a future spaceship will race around Earth grabbing old spacecraft and flinging them back into the atmosphere, though it is hard to imagine a similar clean-up method for the small pieces of debris generated by collisional cascading. Maybe Star Wars technologies will produce a laser that can shoot orbital junk from the sky. But no such technologies are available today. Even if some such technology were developed, it would probably be much more expensive than reserving a bit of fuel to bring a spacecraft down at the end of its functional life.

[19] In 1987 the World Commission on Environment and Development defined sustainable development as meeting the needs of the present generation without compromising the ability of future generations to meet their needs. In space we are failing the sustainability test miserably. A hundred years from now, when our descendants want to put satellites into orbits teeming with debris, they will wonder what we could have been thinking. The simple answer is we weren't thinking at all.

Notes to the Text

1. **The U. S. Space Surveillance Network** (SSN)—a collection of radar and optical sensors used to detect, track and identify objects in space.

2. **NASA**—National Aeronautics and Space Administration, agency of the U. S. government, established by the National Aeronautics and Space Act of 1958. The functions of the organization were conceived to plan, direct, and conduct all U. S. aeronautical and space activities, except those that are primarily military. The administrator of NASA is appointed from civilian life by the president, with the advice and consent of the U. S. Senate. The administration arranges for participation by the scientific community in planning scientific measurements and observations to be made through use of aeronautical and space vehicles and provides for dissemination of information concerning results. Under guidance of the president, the administration participates in the development of programs of international cooperation in space activities. With the advent of the space shuttle program, NASA became more frequently involved in military activities despite its original intent as a civilian agency. Because of the long delay caused by the 1986 *Challenger* disaster, however, the military started expanding its own fleet of booster rockets.

3. **Department of Defense**—executive branch of the United States government, created by Congress in 1949. It is administered by a secretary who is appointed by the president, with the approval of the Senate, and who is a member of the cabinet and the National Security Council. The department directs and controls the armed forces and assists the president in the direction of the nation's security. The major subdivisions are the Office of the Secretary, the Joint Chiefs of Staff, the military departments, the unified and specified commands, the Armed Forces Policy Council, and the agencies.

4. **Challenger accident**—an accident that destroyed the United States space shuttle Challenger 73 seconds after takeoff from the Kennedy Space Center on January 28, 1986. The crew—mission commander Francis R. Scobee; pilot Michael J. Smith; mission specialists Ronald E. McNair,

4

Ellison S. Onizuka, and Judith A. Resnik; and payload specialists Gregory B. Jarvis and Christa McAuliffe, a high school teacher from New Hampshire—died in the accident.

5. **International Space Station**—an internationally developed research facility that is being assembled in low Earth orbit. The objective of the ISS, as defined by NASA, is to develop and test technologies for exploration spacecraft systems, develop techniques to maintain crew health and performance on missions beyond low Earth orbit, and gain operational experience that can be applied to exploration missions. On-orbit construction of the station began in 1998 and is scheduled for completion by mid-2012. The station is expected to remain in operation until at least 2015, and likely 2028.

6. **Space Age**—in October 1957, the former Soviet Union successfully launched Sputnik I, the world's first artificial satellite While the Sputnik launch was a single event, it marked the start of the space age and the U. S. -U. S. S. R space race.

Part I   Comprehension of the Text

1. What is space junk? What are the possible dangers of space junk?
2. What happened that made NASA officials realize the importance of debris research?
3. What is the only effective way to enable a spacecraft to survive impacts with objects in an orbit?
4. Why some of NASA's launch vehicles are left in orbit?
5. Why will it be difficult to make international regulations concerning orbital debris?

Part II   Vocabulary

A. Choose the one from the four choices that best explains the underlined word or phrase.

1. Anyone who is arrested shall be informed at the time of his arrest of the reason for his arrest and shall be <u>promptly</u> informed of any charges against him.
   A. indefinitely   B. strenuously   C. precariously   D. immediately
2. The strong compositions, subtle colors and detailed, elegant decoration of his work, easily <u>lent itself to</u> advertising posters.
   A. applied to   B. gave rise to   C. added up to   D. amounted to
3. The designer wanted to give it a green feel, so we've <u>waived</u> the rules so he can use fake grass as a surface material.
   A. executed   B. abandoned   C. resumed   D. modified
4. It appeared that the rocket <u>blew up</u> at that moment however everything worked out fine and after the second motor ejected a big puff of white smoke.
   A. collapsed   B. smashed   C. exploded   D. immolated
5. Scientists and governments from around the world have reached a <u>consensus</u> about human activity causing global warming.
   A. compromise   B. agreement   C. concession   D. precaution

6. The doctor's assertion caught us by surprise and <u>shattered</u> our dreams like a mortar from the enemy.

    A. spoiled   B. nourished   C. reduced   D. defined

7. Economic growth <u>begets</u> currency strength, and when commodities are booming, so do the currencies of countries reliant on a prosperous commodity sector.

    A. deduces   B. quickens   C. intensifies   D. produces

8. There are clothing requirements for workers who are exposed to the <u>hazards</u> of flames or electric arcs.

    A. defaults   B. deficits   C. dangers   D. disposals

9. Some people think that the relations between people have <u>deteriorated</u> so much that understanding and friendship are almost impossible.

    A. degraded   B. worsened   C. extinguished   D. fragmented

10. He was asked to recopy his composition because it's impossible for the teacher to read his <u>microscopic</u> handwriting.

    A. careless   B. illegible   C. minute   D. untidy

B. Choose the one from the four choices that best completes the sentence.

1. As _____ increases, the atmospheric pressure decreases, thinning the air so that less oxygen is available.

    A. gratitude   B. fortitude   C. altitude   D. latitude

2. Almost every major American city has a restaurant like this—one that _____ with excellent panoramic views of the city.

    A. rotates   B. circulates   C. designates   D. manipulates

3. Satisfaction can _____ from various comparison standards, including predictive expectations, desires, or experience-based norms.

    A. ensure   B. ensue   C. insure   D. pursue

4. The trial of a teenager accused of the murder of a retired psychiatric nurse has been _____ for legal reasons.

    A. vented   B. deserted   C. evaded   D. aborted

5. Health problems _____ a small part of the association between socioeconomic status and disability pension award.

    A. add up to   B. make up for   C. come up to   D. account for

6. Internet experts say home wireless networks can be _____ to repeated use by outside hackers even if they are password-protected.

    A. vulnerable   B. venerable   C. plausible   D. tangible

7. With her understated wit, she has _____ many a bubble of conformity and made audiences laugh in recognition.

    A. patronized   B. pervaded   C. punctured   D. purified

8. These instructions are intended for your use to _____ facial lines and improve skin texture.

    A. diminish   B. deplete   C. disperse   D. dispose

9. Some scientists think average global temperatures have risen due to the greenhouse effect. Others are _____ of global warming.

    A. empirical   B. hysterical   C. ironical   D. skeptical

10. But finally, truth has _____, and what seemed like an impossible dream has been made real by our hard work.

    A. precluded   B. prevailed   C. preceded   D. presided

C. Complete each sentence with the proper form of the word given in the parenthesis.

1. There are at least two _____ consequences inherent with this dramatic change in American philosophy. (escape)

2. Producers say work on the next James Bond film has been halted _____ because of uncertainty about the future of distributor. (definite)

3. Two terrestrial planets orbiting a mature sun-like star some 300 light-years from Earth recently suffered a violent _____. (collide)

4. The _____ of satellites at end-of-life is the only effective means to keep low-Earth orbit clean. (orbit)

5. There are three stages of analysis regarding the _____ distribution of each resource: classification, valuation and distribution. (equity)

6. As we change our environment we change the type of future that awaits us and our _____ and the nature of the planet itself. (descend)

7. While being somewhat technical in nature, this lecture should be accessible to anyone who has even the most _____ knowledge of plant chemistry. (rudiment)

8. A famous theoretical physicist says we should search for Shadow Life, unknown or _____ life forms that may have been hidden on Earth all along. (detect)

9. The following _____ will apply for all flights departing from UK airports on the carriage of liquids and medicines in hand baggage. (restrict)

10. Only if we realize this potential of our humanity can we truly seize the opportunity for global _____. (sustain)

Part III   Cloze

Directions: There are totally 15 blanks in the following passage. Fill each blank with one word only.

In nature, wastes are for the most part returned to the environment through chemical action, bacterial activity and weathering. Some man-made wastes are also processed, or degraded, by these __1__ processes. However, many of the wastes of an industrial society are not readily __2__ and absorbed into the environment and must __3__ special processing. This article deals primarily with the __4__ of the solid portion of man-made wastes, from kitchen garbage to old cars.

For centuries man's nondegradable waste materials have generally been hauled, along with the __5__ wastes, for disposal in open gullies or abandoned pits. This type of disposal has __6__ to a deterioration of the local environment around the dumping sites __7__ the wastes attract insects and

vermin, produce __8__ odors, and sometimes catch fire. The __9__ sites also often mar the natural beauty of the landscape.

Such centers of local __10__ deterioration were multiplying and concentrating rapidly in both developed and developing countries, __11__ because of growing population densities and partly because of the great __12__ in the use of waste-generating goods and services by those concentrated populations. However, because of increasing public concern about the __13__ of the environment, old waste-disposal ways are no longer acceptable in most countries. As a result, some of the old methods are being refined and new ones sought. Since 1968, __14__ a survey revealed that 94% of the land-disposal sites in the United States were inadequate, many states and municipalities have __15__ major strides toward use of sanitary landfill or other improved processing and disposal practices.

Part IV   Writing

Directions:Develop each of the following topics into an essay of about 200 words.

1. Is Space Exploration a Waste of Money?
2. Human Activities and Environment
3. Sustainable Development

Section B   Extensive Reading and Translation

The End Is Not at Hand

By Robert J. Samuelson

[1] Whoever coined the phrase "save the planet" is a public-relations genius. (1) It conveys the sense of impending catastrophe and high purpose that has wrapped environmentalism in an aura of moral urgency. It also typifies environmentalism's rhetorical excesses, which, in any other context, would be seen as wild exaggeration or simple dishonesty.

[2] Up to a point, our environmental awareness has checked a mindless enthusiasm for unrestrained economic growth. We have sensibly curbed some of growth's harmful side effects. (2) But environmentalism increasingly resembles a

holy crusade addicted to hype and ignorant of history. Every environmental ill is depicted as an onrushing calamity that—if not stopped—will end life as we know it.

[3] Take the latest scare: the greenhouse effect. We're presented with the horrifying specter of a world that incinerates itself. Act now, or sizzle later. Food supplies will wither. Glaciers will melt. Coastal areas will flood. In fact, the probable losses from any greenhouse warming are modest: 1 to 2 percent of our economy's output by the year 2050, estimates economist William Cline. The loss seems even smaller compared with the expected growth of the economy (a doubling) over the same period.

[4] No environmental problem threatens the "planet" or rates with the danger of nuclear war. No oil spill ever caused suffering on a par with today's civil war in Yugoslavia, which is a minor episode in human misery. World War II left more than 35 million dead. Cambodia's civil war resulted in 1 million to 3 million deaths. The great scourges of humanity remain what they have always been: war, natural disaster, oppressive government, crushing poverty and hate. On any scale of tragedy, environmental distress is a featherweight.

[5] This is not an argument for indifference or inaction. It is an argument for perspective and balance. You can believe (as I do) that the possibility of greenhouse warming enhances an already strong case for an energy tax. A tax would curb ordinary air pollution, limit oil imports, cut the budget deficit and promote energy-efficient investments that make economic sense.

[6] But it does not follow that anyone who disagrees with me is evil or even wrong. On the greenhouse effect, for instance, there's ample scientific doubt over whether warming will occur and, if so, how much. Moreover, the warming would occur over decades. People and businesses could adjust. To take one example: farmers could shift to more heat-resistant seeds.

[7] Unfortunately, the impulse of many environmentalists is to vilify and simplify. Critics of environmental restrictions are portrayed as selfish and ignorant creeps. Doomsday scenarios are developed to prove the seriousness of environmental dangers. Cline's recent greenhouse study projected warming 250 years into the future. Guess what, it increases sharply. This is an absurd exercise akin to predicting life in 1992 at the time of the French and Indian War (1754—1763).

[8] The rhetorical overkill is not just innocent excess. It clouds our understanding. For starters, it minimizes the great progress that has been made especially in industrialized countries. In the United States, air and water pollution have dropped dramatically. Since 1960, particulate emissions (soot, cinders) are down by 65 percent. Lead emissions have fallen by 97 percent since 1970. Smog has declined in most cities.

[9] What's also lost is the awkward necessity for choices. Your environmental benefit may be my job. Not every benefit is worth having at any cost. Economists estimate that environmental regulations depress the economy's output by 2.6 to 5 percent, or about $150 billion to $290 billion. (Note: this is larger than the estimated impact of global warming.) (3) For that cost, we've lowered health risks and improved our surroundings. But some gains are small compared with the costs. And some costs are needlessly high because regulations are rigid.

[10] The worst sin of environmental excess is its bias against economic growth. The cure for the immense problems of poor countries usually lies with economic growth. A recent report from the World Bank estimates that more than 1 billion people lack healthy water supplies and sanitary facilities. The result is hundreds of millions of cases of diarrhea annually and the deaths of 3 million children (2 million of which the World Bank judges avoidable). Only by becoming wealthier can countries correct these conditions.

[11] Similarly, wealthier societies have both the desire and the income to clean their air and water. Advanced nations have urban-air-pollution levels only a sixth that of the poorest countries. Finally, economic growth tends to reduce high birthrates, as children survive longer and women escape traditional roles.

[12] Yes, we have environmental problems. Reactors in the former Soviet Union pose safety risks. Economic growth and the environment can be at odds. (4) Growth generates carbon-dioxide emissions and causes more waste. But these problems are not—as environmental rhetoric implies—the main obstacles to sustained development. The biggest hurdle is inept government. Inept government fostered unsafe Soviet reactors. Inept government hampers food production in poor countries by, say, preventing farmers from earning adequate returns on their crops.

[13] By now, everyone is an environmentalist. (5) But the label is increasingly meaningless, because not all environmental problems are equally serious and even the serious ones need to be balanced against other concerns. Environmentalism should hold the hype. It should inform us more and frighten us less.

Part A Translate English into Chinese

I. Translate the underlined sentences in the above text into Chinese.

II. Translate paragraphs 4—6 in the above text into Chinese.

Part B Translate Chinese into English

I. Translate the following sentences into English with the words or phrases in the passage in Section B.

1. 中国政府近期就汽车以旧换新补贴政策公开征求意见,汽车以旧换新是刺激个人消费、减少污染的系列措施之一。

2. 这些被称为彩虹玫瑰或开心玫瑰的多色花花期也和普通玫瑰一样长,只是它们的枝叶会迅速凋谢。

3. 小心遵守所有的道路规则,就能把开车的危险减少到最低限度。

4. 温暖、下沉的空气能够阻碍云的形成,致使降雨减少,空气和土壤的湿度降低。

5. 那小夫妻俩过了五年的吵闹生活,最后终于分道扬镳了。

II. Translate the following paragraph into English.

　　美国的金融危机已成为席卷全球的经济危机,中国作为世界经济的一部分,经济发展和节能减排受到巨大冲击。纵观历史重大危机事件,均对经济发展产生巨大负面影响,而对能源消耗和污染物排放,则有巨大的节能减排效用。中国的经济增长和节能减排目标雄心勃勃,"十一五"规划的各项措施均严格按要求得以执行,但从过去三年实际结果来看,节能减排似乎不尽如人意。然而从 2008 年 8 月开始,经济增长放缓,能源消费迅速下滑,节能减排似乎不再成为首要难题,但这只是暂时的。随着经济的复苏,能源消费和污染物排放迅速反弹。从长远看,经济必将不断增长,节能减排是一项长远的战略性挑战,不可掉以轻心。

Unit 5

Section A   Intensive Reading and Writing

How to Increase Your Mental Potential

By John H. Douglas

According to new research, intelligence involves a host of skills that ordinary people can consciously enhance.

[1] The teenager had crushing news for his parents. Slow from infancy, troublesome in school, he was now capping his academic failures with a disgraceful expulsion order: "Your presence in class is disruptive and affects the other students".

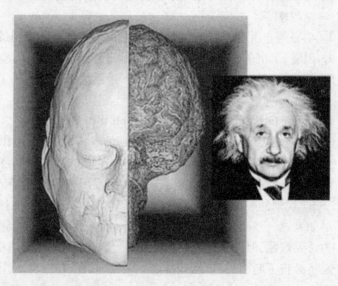

[2] Years later, he recalled his learning problems philosophically: "My intellectual development was retarded, as a result of which I began to wonder about space and time only when I had already grown up. Naturally, I could go deeper into the problem than a child". And so, 11 years after expulsion from school, young Albert Einstein[1] published the theory of relativity that changed our understanding of the universe.

[3] No one in this century has been more widely recognized as a genius than Einstein. Yet his problems with early intellectual development and his peculiar gifts cast great doubt on all our conventional ideas about genius, intelligence or "I. Q.[2]". On the one hand, Einstein showed early defects in abilities that our mental tests value; on the other hand, his special intellectual faculties went far beyond most definitions of intelligence. Moreover, their growth appears peculiarly gradual, contradicting the popular conception of intelligence as something inborn and fixed. Aptitudes that he had learned rather than inherited—particularly his dogged persistence and his skills in playing games with ideas—were apparently as crucial to his genius as any cutting edge of intellect.

[4] These powerful aspects of intelligence that conventional definitions overlook are getting close

attention in a new wave of research. This comes after years of earlier studies exposed the narrowness of our usual measures of mental aptitude. Intelligence, it turns out, is multifaceted and marvelous; it includes personality traits, creativity skills and intellectual wizardries that show up on no test.

[5] What is most exciting is that some of these ill-defined abilities are possessed by many people. Just knowing about such neglected skills will help us discover and nurture untapped potential in ourselves and in our children. A better understanding of these abilities is emerging from research along four major lines:

[6] (1) Intellectual Quotient. I. Q. test scores are not as important as once believed. Long-term studies show that the scores may vary considerably over a person's lifetime, and their value as predictors of success in school has been vastly overrated. According to recent studies, I. Q. accounts for only about 35 to 45 percent of the variation in students' academic performance. More than half still remains unexplained. Moreover, studies demonstrate that success in school is a poor predictor of success in later life.

[7] New research also indicates that reasoning ability, an aspect of intelligence that I. Q. tests do measure, can be trained in ways that help students do better in school. Experimental preschool programs have helped raise the scholastic ability of slum children, for example. And psychologists Arthur and Linda Shaw Whimbey assert that any healthy person can learn abstract reasoning skills. They have helped college students make better grades through a training program described in their book *Intelligence Can Be Taught*. Large vocabularies, which are learned, usually correlate with high scores on I. Q. tests, as does reading comprehension, a skill stressed in I. Q. training programs.

[8] Many such programs view the I. Q. variables of intelligence as a particular psychological "set"—a problem-solving readiness. Obviously, this can be trained, just as physical readiness for competitive sports can be trained.

[9] (2) Creativity. I. Q. scores, which reflect ability to home in on a single correct answer through logical steps, measure only about a half-dozen variables of mental ability. "Creativity tests", which involve adeptness at finding many solutions to a problem, measure perhaps a dozen more. Between the two, only about one-sixth of the specific abilities believed to be involved in intelligence are explored. Creativity is just another aspect of intelligence, by itself almost as narrow as I. Q.

[10] (3) Personality. Individuals who achieve greatness in some intellectual endeavor usually do so through force of personality as much as through sheer smartness. In the past, narrow definitions of intelligence usually excluded personality factors. Today, scientists studying persons who have demonstrated outstanding intellectual accomplishment have found they differ from ordinary people in several personality traits. In addition to curiosity, persistence and capacity for self-criticism—qualities that Einstein had—highly creative people also show an unusual openness, independence, imaginativeness and playfulness.

[11] (4) Brain structure and chemistry. Advances in our knowledge of brain physiology may help us understand some of the dozens of other intellectual faculties not measured by I. Q., creativity or personality tests. For example, attention—so fundamental to guided intellectual effort—is largely governed by the more primitive regions of the brain that also control emotions. And the link between emotional involvement with a subject and one's ability to comprehend it appears to be a chemical

"reward system" located in the brain, in which the emotions reward the attention center for a job well done—creating a feeling of satisfaction and well-being.

[12] The implications of these four broad areas of research are serious. By concentrating mainly on I. Q. tests alone, schools have often rejected students whose strengths lie in other sorts of mental ability. As one leader in the field of ability testing, E. Paul Torrance, puts it, "If we identify (talented) children only on the basis of intelligence tests, we eliminate approximately 70 percent of the most creative".

[13] The point is that the majority of us shine in some facets of mental ability. Some people are better than others at problem solving, others excel at originality, still others succeed at mental tasks requiring persistence. All these traits are key components of human intelligence. To discover and develop your own kind of "smarts", try asking questions like these:

What do I like working with: words or numbers, abstract concepts or concrete ideas?

Am I better at dealing with people or things, and why?

When I'm explaining something, do I draw pictures, use words, or do I prefer to act things out?

Faced with a new situation, do I tend to memorize things or figure them out?

For fun, would I rather solve puzzles or make up stories?

Am I better at grasping the specific relationship between things or at seeing the whole picture?

Given a choice between two jobs, would I take the one demanding quick action or the one requiring patience?

[14] Depending on the problem at hand, any combination of these diverse skills could add up to being "smart". A marriage counselor, for example, had better be good at working with people, determining relationships and evaluating courses of action. On the other hand, a physicist needs to feel comfortable manipulating numbers, solving puzzles and glimpsing a larger vision of nature from scanty threads of data.

[15] Intelligence can be developed, but it takes effort. The first step is to capitalize on the kind of smarts you already have while trying to improve the rest. Often this involves a change of thinking habits and looking at the world around you in a new way.

[16] To understand the process better, let's look at some methods used by people respected for their intelligence. They have adopted positive thinking habits. They welcome challenging problems and try to learn from each new situation. They have the courage to defend their ideas. The best, like Einstein, manage to balance urgent motivation with patience enough to see a project through. That's a tall order, but here are some ways each of us can improve our own intelligence:

[17] Adopt a systematic approach to problem solving. One of the most common traits among students who score poorly on I. Q. tests is impulsiveness, which leads them to guess at answers without thinking through a problem thoroughly. Practice solving problems by breaking them down into a series of steps.

[18] Master the many skills of reading. A critical element in most I. Q. tests involves being able to identify relationships between words, a skill that can be mastered only through much reading—paying particular attention to unfamiliar words and how they are used. Anyone who has ever had the experience of adding a powerful new word to his vocabulary or a new logical idea to his

understanding, and has then found it helpful in analyzing, discriminating and problem solving, knows the satisfaction that comes with expanded mental ability.

[19] Develop a thoughtful environment for yourself and your children. Research on productive people shows they have been encouraged to entertain original, even "wild" ideas, without fear of ridicule; wherever an environment threatens a person with immediate rejection of some new idea—whether at the dinner table, in a classroom or in a repressive society—original thinking suffers.

[20] It seems likely that certain subjects or mental activities such as logic, or math, or poetry—will exercise reasoning skills more than other activities (such as watching television). A thoughtful environment is not only full of support but free from distraction.

[21] The secret of intellectual success is realizing that no one trait or ability is sufficient. A high I. Q. is lost unless supported by perseverance and empathy. Imagination and openness to new ideas—what most people call common sense—can contribute as much as I. Q. to your success.

Notes to the Text

1. **Albert Einstein** (1879—1955)—American theoretical physicist (born in Germany of Jewish parents), known for the formulation of the relativity theory. He is recognized as one of the greatest physicists of all time. He was an examiner (1902—1907) in the Swiss patent office in Bern. During this period he obtained his doctorate from the University of Zurich, evolved the Special Theory of Relativity, explained the photoelectric effect, and studied the motion of atoms. For his work in theoretical physics, notably on the photo-electric effect, he received the 1921 Nobel Prize in physics. His property was confiscated (1934) by the Nazi Government, and he was deprived of his German citizenship. In 1940 he became an American citizen.

2. **I. Q.** —intelligence quotient, a term devised by American psychologist Lewis Madison Terman (1877—1956). It is an index of measurement of the intelligence level of both children and adults, with a normal standard of 100. It is the mental age (as shown by intelligence tests) multiplied by 100 and divided by the chronological age.

Part I　Comprehension of the Text

1. What can be concluded from Einstein's intellectual development?
2. According to the author, what affects the IQ test scores?
3. What should a person do before he makes effort to increase his mental potential?
4. Why does it take effort to develop one's intelligence?
5. What ways are there that can be used to increase one's intelligence?

Part II Vocabulary

A. Choose the one from the four choices that best explains the underlined word or phrase.

1. In today's competitive job market, graduates need to <u>enhance</u> their degree with skills and experiences that will give them an edge over other candidates.

    A. strengthen   B. reinforce   C. heighten   D. solidify

2. He is an effective mediator and facilitator <u>adept</u> at communication and interpersonal challenges and conflict resolution system development.

    A. capable   B. skilled   C. competent   D. fluent

3. Water has long been known to exhibit many physical properties that <u>discriminate</u> it from other small molecules of comparable mass.

    A. disintegrate   B. distinguish   C. disorientate   D. disseminate

4. Located at single points, along lines, or on whole surfaces in the solid, these <u>defects</u> influence its mechanical, electrical, and optical behavior.

    A. deceits   B. errands   C. faults   D. genres

5. Happiness cannot be taught by any teacher or spiritual guide unless we ourselves decide to be happy and make an <u>endeavor</u> to find our own ways to be happy.

    A. effect   B. esteem   C. excess   D. effort

6. Interactive music mixers allow the user to <u>manipulate</u> sound samples and sound loops that can be mixed and matched to create a song.

    A. multiply   B. improve   C. handle   D. utilize

7. Men go for the glory, and women do all the small things that <u>add up to</u> something really special.

    A. amount   B. signify   C. distribute   D. designate

8. They create their own mythical dragons by hybridizing two creatures with desirable <u>traits</u> and writing stories about their creation.

    A. virtues   B. merits   C. characters   D. features

9. Rather than regretting the loss of structure, he <u>capitalized on</u> the opportunities that arise when the strictures of tradition are loosened.

    A. kept abreast of   B. took advantage of   C. lost track of   D. took account of

10. Innovation is a crucial <u>component</u> of business strategy, but the process of innovation may seem difficult to manage.

    A. ingredient   B. segment   C. digestant   D. detergent

B. Choose the one from the four choices that best completes the sentence.

1. Scientists have shown that traces of blood in various materials are _____ completely when they are washed with detergents containing active oxygen.

    A. retarded   B. eliminated   C. demolished   D. dissolved

2. This position requires problem solving skills, an _____ for accuracy and detail, and the ability to work independently and cooperate with all levels of staff and the public.

A. aptitude   B. attribute   C. altitude   D. attitude

3. We can usually learn much more from people whose views we share than from people whose views _____ our own.

A. contribute   B. illuminate   C. contradict   D. exclude

4. The present invention relates to an unmanned underwater vehicle for tracking and _____ submarines.

A. catching up with   B. keeping pace with   C. falling back on   D. homing in on

5. You should be the first one to _____ your own work before you show it to a friend or relative for review, or turn it in to a teacher for grading.

A. estimate   B. evaluate   C. appreciate   D. overrate

6. Like other famous rivers all over the world, Yangtze River, with fantastic sceneries and a long history, has _____ brilliant civilization in south China.

A. nurtured   B. ventured   C. tortured   D. fractured

7. We know that a customer's understanding of their benefits is _____ to how much they trust us as their health service company.

A. coincided   B. correlated   C. integrated   D. combined

8. The documents were not signed, which cast _____ on their authenticity, so they should not be admitted by the court.

A. doubt   B. light   C. shadow   D. ridicule

9. The microorganisms that _____ organic matter into compost need some water to live, but if there is too much water, they won't have enough oxygen.

A. break off   B. break up   C. break away   D. break down

10. As she read to the class, the teacher had each child _____ a different character in the story.

A. figure out   B. turn out   C. act out   D. make out

C. Complete each sentence with the proper form of the word given in the parenthesis.

1. Jeff Weinberger has spent more than 20 years helping companies create, adapt to and capitalize on _____ change in their markets, technologies and businesses. (disrupt)

2. It is a traditional school practice to use suspension and _____ as possible punishments for students. But tradition does not justify bad practice. (expel)

3. Mr. Smith did not attend Tuesday's hearing but pleaded no contest to _____ conduct and incompetence through his lawyer. (grace)

4. A study on cancer against age will also have to take into account _____ such as income, location, stress, and lifestyle. (vary)

5. The administration has deliberately fomented tensions between the groups in order to justify its _____ political measures. (repress)

6. She brings an _____, intelligence and vitality with her and gives the text that special touch, but also a special desire to play the role. (impulse)

7. The difference between _____ and obstinacy is that one often comes from a strong will and the other from a strong won't. (persevere)

8. The faculty of memory is not at all limited by the amount one has _____ ; on the contrary, it is an expansive faculty. (memory)

9. For more than two decades, we have sparked _____ learning with our unique brand of engaging and educational live programs and activities. (imagine)

10. It is generally accepted that postgraduate research projects must demonstrate a degree of _____ and a degree of analysis. (origin)

Part III Cloze

Directions: There are totally 15 blanks in the following passage. Fill each blank with one word only.

Why people who are emotionally intelligent succeed while those with merely a moderate IQ considerably fail? First we need to understand that emotional intelligence (EQ) is not the opposite of IQ; EQ is actually __1__ to IQ resembled in academic intelligence and cognitive skills, and studies actually show that our __2__ states affect the way our brain functions as well as its processing speed. Studies have even shown that Albert Einstein's superior __3__ ability may have been linked to the part of the brain that supports __4__ functions. The natures of EQ and IQ __5__ however in the ability to learn and develop them. IQ is a __6__ potential that is established at birth and happens to be __7__ after a certain age (pre-puberty) and can not be developed nor increased after then. EQ __8__ can be learned, developed and improved at any age, and studies have actually shown that our ability to learn emotional intelligence __9__ as we get older. Another difference is that IQ is a threshold __10__ that can only show you the road to your career and gets you working in a certain field __11__ it is EQ that walks through that road and gets you promoted in that field. __12__ , striking a balance between IQ and EQ is an important element of managerial success. For some extent, IQ is a driver of productive performance; __13__ IQ-based competencies are considered "threshold abilities", i. e. the skills needed for you to do an average job. __14__ , EQ-based competencies and skills are by far more effective, especially at higher levels of organizations __15__ IQ differences are negligible. Dr. Goleman says that even though organizations are different, have different needs, it was found that EQ contributed by 80% ~ 90% of predicting success in organizations in general.

1. A. complementary   B. complimentary   C. supplementary   D. contemporary

2. A. intellectual   B. intelligent   C. emotional   D. emotive

3. A. cognitive   B. intelligent   C. intellectual   D. creative

4. A. physiological   B. psychological   C. biological   D. psychiatrical

5. A. resemble   B. assemble   C. support   D. differ

6. A. mental   B. ethnic   C. psychic   D. genetic

7. A. fixed   B. varied   C. various   D. flexed

8. A. in comparison   B. on the contrary   C. in addition   D. at length

9. A. decreases   B. diminishes   C. increases   D. descends

10. A. capability   B. performance   C. capacitance   D. qualification

11. A. because   B. but   C. since   D. as

12. A. However   B. Moreover   C. Therefore   D. Furthermore

13. A. hence   B. though   C. while   D. however

14. A. On the other hand   B. By contrast   C. What's more   D. In turn

15. A. when   B. where   C. because   D. although

Part IV   Writing

Directions: Develop each of the following topics into an essay of about 200 words.

1. Success in school is a poor predictor of success in later life. Do you agree? Explain.

2. Individuals who achieve greatness in some intellectual endeavor usually do so through force of personality as much as through sheer smartness. In your opinion, what are the important personality traits that will enable a person to succeed? Explain.

3. A high I. Q. is lost unless supported by perseverance and empathy. Interpret your understanding of the statement.

Section B   Extensive Reading and Translation

Why Smart People Fail?

By Carole Hyatt and Linda Gottlieb

[1] You have probably failed sometime in your career. (1) After all, the only way to avoid failure is never to strive for success, to remain fixed where you are. But you can learn from failure, figure out what went wrong and correct it. You have the power to change.

[2] Even someone as successful as Samuel Beckett, perhaps the 20th century's preeminent playwright, once wrote that he felt at home with failure, "having breathed deep of its vivifying air".

[3] Scrutiny of defeat is critical. You have to confront your failure to avoid repeating it. Based on almost 200 interviews with people who survived major career defeats, here are the six most common reasons for failure. Whether you are a corporate executive or a civic volunteer, you might find yourself in this list.

[4] **Lack of social skills.** Most people who fail for this reason talk of "office politics" doing them in, but the politics may be nothing more than normal interactions among people. If you have trouble with "office politics", you may really be having trouble dealing with people.

[5] You may get along on brilliance alone for a while, but most careers involve other people. You can have great academic intelligence and still lack social intelligence—the ability to be a good listener, to be sensitive toward others, to give and take criticism well. People with high social intelligence admit their mistakes, take their share of blame and move on. They know how to build team support.

[6] If people don't like you, they may help you fail. One day at an airport, a traveler observed a well-dressed businessman yelling at a porter about the porter's handling of his luggage. The more abusive the businessman became, the calmer the porter seemed. After the businessman left, the traveler complimented the porter on his restraint. "Oh, that's nothing", he said, smiling. "You know, that man's going to Miami, but his bags—they are going to Kalamazoo." Co-workers—even subordinates—if poorly treated, can do you in.

[7] On the other hand, you can get away with serious mistakes if you are socially intelligent. This is why many mediocre executives survive violent corporate upheavals. Sensitive in their dealings with others, they are well liked; when they make mistakes, their supporters usually help them

recover. A mistake may actually further their careers if the boss thinks they handled the situation in a mature and responsible way.

[8] (2) People with poor interpersonal skills have trouble taking criticism. When confronted with a mistake, they left their ego and emotions get in the way. They may deny responsibility and become moody, volatile or angry. They mark themselves as "prickly" and "temperamental".

[9] Social intelligence is an acquired skill. The more you practice, the better you get. Like good manners, it can be learned.

[10] **Wrong fit.** You may not have failed at all. You may simply be suffering a case of mismatch. Success requires fitting your abilities, interests, personality, style and values with your work.

[11] David Brown, one of the most successful movie producers in America, was fired from three corporate jobs before he figured out that corporate life was not for him. (3) In Hollywood he rose to become No. 2 at twentieth Century Fox, until he recommended the film Cleopatra, which turned out to be a commercial disaster. Layoffs followed. He was fired.

[12] In New York, he became an editorial vice president at New American Library, but the owners brought in an outsider with whom he clashed. Brown was fired.

[13] Back in California, he was reinstated at twentieth Century Fox and was in the top echelon there for six years. But the board of directors decided they didn't like some pictures he had recommended. Once again, he was fired, along with Fox's president, Richard D. Zanuck.

[14] Brown began to examine his working behavior. (4) The way he operated in corporations —being out-spoken, risk-oriented, eager to move on his own instincts—was more the style of an owner than an employee. He hated committee management and the corporate mentality.

[15] Analysis of failure made Brown and Zanuck go out on their own and produce the Sting, Jaws, the Verdict, and Cocoon. Brown wasn't a failed corporate executive; he was a hidden entrepreneur.

[16] For some people the key value is risk, and they suffer from wrong fit in a staid corporate culture. For others the core value is doing something worthwhile; these people are likely to sabotage themselves if they are not in a mission-oriented job.

[17] **Absence of commitment.** One lawyer we interviewed readily admits, "I really haven't achieved my expectations". No wonder. He cushions himself against failure by never really trying. If he doesn't put himself on the line, he can always tell himself, I didn't really care about that so much anyway.

[18] After graduating from a prestigious law school, he joined a large firm out west, hoping to specialize in the entertainment department. Somehow it never happened. As a result, he says, "I behaved in an in-between fashion, not telling off the senior partners, but not doing a really good job either".

[19] He moved to the East Coast and joined a corporate law firm. Six months later he was asked to leave because he seemed to lack motivation. "It didn't bother me. I didn't like the firm anyway", he says. At present he is practicing entertainment law but is forever discontented. "Let's face it", he says, "this is the minor leagues".

[20] The imaginary terrors of failure loom so large that non-committers try to prevent failure by not involving themselves emotionally. Of course, what they're doing by their halfhearted actions is increasing the likelihood of their downfall.

[21] Lack of self-esteem is a basic cause of failure. To be committed—indeed, to be successful at anything—you have to believe you can do it. Employers search for this as much as any other job qualification. People who lack self-esteem, although they may say all the right things, often say them with a question mark in their voices.

[22] You can get better at projecting a sense of self-esteem—even if you don't really feel it. Like an actor in a play, monitor your voice and actions to be sure you sound self-confident. Tape-record an imaginary interview and listen to yourself.

[23] **Too scattered a focus.** Some people do so many things that they end up doing none of them well. One real-estate entrepreneur in our study reached the point that he could no longer remember how many deals he was involved with. He started with one building, which led to two buildings, which led to getting more credit and extending himself into other types of businesses. "It was exciting", he recalls, "I was testing the limits of my capabilities".

[24] One day the bank informed him that he was overextended and his credit was ended. The boy wonder had failed.

[25] At first he blamed everybody else—the banks, the economy, his staff. Finally, he says, "I realized I'd gone too far, too fast". By trying to do everything, he had lost focus and failed to set priorities. Whatever problem screamed most loudly for his attention that day was the one he would attend to.

[26] The answer was to refocus, to sort out what he did best—real-estate development. He went through several lean years, but he gradually rebuilt. Today he is once again a successful businessman—with a clearer sense of his limits.

[27] Recognizing your limitations, establishing priorities and organizing your ventures are essential to success.

[28] Why do smart people fail? They can fail for many reasons. (5) But failure is not the point —the best of people experience that. It is learning from failure that is special. The distinguishing characteristic about really smart people? They learn.

Part A   Translate English into Chinese

I. Translate the underlined sentences in the above text into Chinese.

II. Translate paragraphs 4, 5, 20 and 21 in the above text into Chinese.

Part B Translate Chinese into English

I. Translate the following sentences into English with the words or phrases in the passage in Section B.

1. 1979 年 11 月,在国际奥委会主席的帮助下,中国在国际奥委会中的地位得到了恢复。

2. 在最初的几个月里,我密切监测它的健康状况,大约每两周就带它去看一次兽医。

3. 主人就像拥抱一个老朋友一样拥抱了他,并对他穿的衣服赞美了一番。

4. 历史证明无限制地、缺乏监督地行使权力不可避免地会导致腐败。

5. 父母应给孩子更多的机会去认识世界、体验生活,从而增强他们独立克服困难、解决问题的综合能力。

II. Translate the following paragraph into English.

与许多人的看法背道而驰,极为聪明的儿童并非注定在学业上取得成功。事实上,所谓的天才生可能超乎寻常的聪明但未能做到学业有成。尽管聪明孩子在低年级时因为功课容易,不必努力学习,但当课程难度加大时,因为没有付出努力去学习,他们可能学得很吃力,表现也不佳,有些情形是由于以前从未认真学习过,他们可能不知道该如何学习。其他情形则是他们根本不能接受有些任务需要付出努力这一事实。

Unit 6

Section A Intensive Reading and Writing

What Makes Sony Run

By Christopher Lucas

[1] Sony began in 1946 in a fire-bombed Tokyo department store with 20 workers and $500 capital. Today the company employs over 40,000 people, and its annual sales reach almost $5 billion. It now sells more than 10,000 different models of sound and video equipment in more than 180 countries on six continents. Sony is Japan's 69th biggest company, yet its reputation as a pioneer (transistor radios), and its influence as a trendsetter (walk-about stereo), make it hard to equal. Add

imagination, grinding hard work, fiercely motivated managers and innovative engineers and designers, and the company seems almost impossible to beat.

[2] Sony's founders, Masaru Ibuka[1] and Akio Morita[2], both physicists, still run the corporation. They are not only partners but lifelong friends who complement each other. Ibuka, now 76, is shy, professorial, the inventor; Morita, 63, is dynamic, extroverted, the super-salesman. Both are extraordinarily intuitive. They have called the world's markets correctly for almost three decades, while their persistence and good taste have almost single-handedly changed the world's opinion of "Made in Japan" from contempt to adulation.

[3] Ibuka and Morita met during the final months of World War II. They joined forces at war's end, incorporating as Tokyo Telecommunications Engineering Co., Ltd[3]. From the start, Ibuka had a dream to apply a mix of electronics and engineering to consumer goods. Within six months the company was making ends meet with the production of vacuumtube voltmeters.

[4] When Ibuka and Morita switched to complex broadcasting consoles, business was so good they were forced to move to bigger quarters—a group of shacks in the suburb of Shinagawa[4], site of

Sony's present-day headquarters. But Ibuka and Morita still didn't have their hoped-for unique consumer product. Then Ibuka saw an American-made tape recorder at the Japan Broadcasting Corporation.

[5] At the time, in the late 1940's, tape recorders were virtually unknown in Japan. But the partners perceived their potential and snapped up the Japanese patent. The recorder's electronic technology presented no problem; but the magnetic tape proved a real headache: there wasn't any in Japan. So Ibuka and Morita invented their own. Since no plastic was available either, and cellophane didn't work, they used ordinary paper, spraying it with magnetic iron powder from an airbrush. Within a year all was ready and Ibuka and Morita had a unique product for a wide-open market.

[6] But at first few people would buy it. Morita realized that scientific creativity was not enough. Customers simply didn't know what to do with their wonderful new machine. He would have to educate them. Morita concluded that the recorder's best market in Japan would be in its schools, and set off around Japan's schools, showing teachers how they could use the portable suitcase-size machine to tape educational radio programs and for English-language lessons. Within 18 months, 30 percent of Japan's elementary schools had bought tape recorders. Then came the avalanche: banks, offices, universities, Japan's broadcasting network—everybody wanted a tape recorder.

[7] In 1952 Ibuka heard of an intriguing new gadget called the transistor, developed by Bell Laboratories[5], and he flew to the United States to investigate. "Radios!" he kept repeating on his return. "We're going to use this transistor to make small, portable radios for everyone!"

[8] Ibuka's conviction fired the imagination of everybody in the company. Morita dashed to America to scoop up all available tidbits of transistor information. The technology was new and utterly unintelligible, but the partners plunged in anyway.

[9] Within several weeks the company successfully produced its first transistor. Inventing its own technology, Ibuka's team soon produced the world's first pocket-size transistor radio—about two years ahead of all Japanese competitors.

[10] For the pocket radio's brand name, the two founders settled on Sony, from the Latin sonus (sound) plus a touch of sonny. ("We were still a couple of sonny boys", says Morita.) Short, identifiable, easy to pronounce, Sony became the company's name too.

[11] In 1956 Morita decided to crack the U. S. market, and flew to New York with his transistor radio. American buyers were fascinated with Sony's invention, and Morita was soon taking orders for 10,000 and more. In February 1960 Sony Corporation of America, the first wholly owned Japanese subsidiary in the United States, opened for business in New York City. Morita himself moved to New York to spearhead the operation—a first for any senior Japanese executive—and within three months he had a sales network covering half the country. Sony America hasn't looked back since—its business was worth well over $ 1.3 billion in 1983.

[12] From the laboratories and factories in Japan, meanwhile, came a breathtaking list of firsts: an AM/FM transistor radio, a five-inch transistorized TV, a desktop calculator, a transistor video tape recorder, a Trinitron[6] color TV set, a Betamax[7] video tape-recorder (VTR) system, a Walkman portable stereo, a still video camera, a typewriter that records both voice and print and a flat micro-TV.

[13] How does Sony do it? The company's greatest secret is its ability to satisfy unvoiced desires. Ibuka, Morita and their staff sense a need, fill it, and then explain it to the public. And in this evolution, Sony frequently and unashamedly adapts or perfects processes invented by others, while simultaneously dipping into its own dazzling bank of advanced technology.

[14] To see how fast the process can work, consider the development of the highly successful Sony Walkman. The walkman began when a few audio engineers tinkered with their company's portable dictation machine. Out of curiosity, they converted it into a four-track stereo recorder, and then connected this to an ordinary pair of headphones. To their amazement, the sound was superb. It was July 1979.

[15] Next day Ibuka wandered in, spotted the contraption, and was instantly intrigued. Still, he thought the bulky headphones should be replaced with featherweight ones the company was already developing.

[16] Designers and engineers were put on a top-priority footing to complete the design and specifications. Soon they returned with a machine that had 204 parts and weighed just under 14 ounces. Factories were readied, production lines assembled, advertising, packaging and naming discussed. Walkman was launched in Japan only five months from its inception! Sony is now producing three million walkmans a year.

[17] Besides inspired use of its scientific talent and know-how, Sony is backed by highly innovative management. Intertwining the best of East and West, the Sony spirit starts at the top with Ibuka and Morita, who are leaders rather than bosses. And unlike most companies, Sony revels in hiring people with contrasting personalities and back-grounds. Sony does not hire able people to fill a specific position; rather, each is hired as a person, for what he or she is and will be. Then employees are goaded and pushed into the most challenging jobs they can handle. The job is tailored to the person, not vice versa.

[18] As a result of these innovative management practices, Sony is an intensely lively, feisty organization that prides itself on personal excellence as much as traditional company loyalty, on individual creativity as much as group effort. Masaru Ibuka and Akio Morita have plunged over and over into the risky, exciting world of advanced high technology, pioneering the new and the unknown. Sony's managers and scientists know what they're doing, and they can prove they're right. Nothing succeeds like success. And that's what makes Sony run.

Excerpts from Reader's Digest

Notes to the Text

1. **Masaru Ibuka** (井深大, April 11, 1908, Nikko City, Japan—December 19, 1997, Tokyo)—a Japanese electronics industrialist. He co-founded what is now Sony.
2. **Akio Morita** (盛田昭夫, January 26, 1921, Nagoya, Aichi—October 3, 1999, Tokyo)—a Japanese businessman and co-founder of Sony Corporation along with Masaru Ibuka.
3. Tokyo Telecommunications Engineering Co., Ltd.: 东京通讯有限公司, Co. = Company, Ltd. = Limited 股份有限公司, 相当于(美) Inc. = Incorporated.

6

4. **Shinagawa**（品川区）—one of the 23 special wards of Tokyo, Japan. In English, it is called Shinagawa City. The ward is home to nine embassies.

5. **Bell Laboratories**—(also known as **Bell Labs** and formerly known as **AT&T Bell Laboratories** and **Bell Telephone Laboratories**) is the research and development subsidiary of the French-owned Alcatel-Lucent and previously of the American Telephone & Telegraph Company（AT&T）. Bell Laboratories operates its headquarters at Murray Hill, New Jersey, United States, and has research and development facilities throughout the world.

6. Trinitron：单枪三束彩色显像管。

7. Betamax：索尼磁带录像机所用制式的名称,另一种其他厂家常用的制式为 VHS。

Part I   Comprehension of the Text

1. Why does Sony seem almost impossible to beat?

2. When was "Sony" used as the company's name? And why?

3. Was it easy for Sony Company to enter the US market?

4. What are the secrets for Sony's great success?

5. What makes Sony a very lively, energetic organization?

Part II   Vocabulary

A. Choose the one from the four choices that best explains the underlined word or phrase.

1. Holmes was so covered with the <u>adulation</u> of his admirers that he has almost disappeared as an actual human being.

   A. excessive praise   B. favorable comment   C. proper compliment   D. slight admiration

2. Ethical considerations should be <u>incorporated</u> into decision-making about public health issues.

   A. integrated   B. included   C. combined   D. excluded

3. Cosmology, the study of the universe as a whole, has <u>intrigued</u> people since they first started looking at the skies.

   A. provoked   B. deceived   C. entertained   D. interested

4. Harlin moved from Europe to America, and, with an insatiable sense of wanderlust, he <u>reveled in</u> downhill skiing and rock-climbing.

   A. enjoyed   B. abandoned   C. improved   D. persisted

5. The United States plans to study the possibility of using mixed-oxide fuel <u>converted</u> from nuclear-weapon material to operate two nuclear power plants.

   A. separated   B. generated   C. changed   D. distinguished

6. As more plants close and fewer workers are needed to <u>assemble</u> cars, fewer dealers are needed to sell those cars.

   A. string together   B. gather together   C. collect together   D. put together

7. Roy bent down and <u>scooped up</u> all the leaves on the ground, palming them in his hand and placing them roughly in his pocket.

    A. gathered   B. accumulated   C. converged   D. scattered

8. The global war on terror, <u>spearheaded</u> by the United States since September. 11, 2001, has seen ongoing tensions between military, political expediencies.

    A. motivated   B. triggered   C. pioneered   D. initiated

9. Research suggests that people trying to quit drinking experience more cognitive improvements when they <u>simultaneously</u> stop smoking.

    A. nevertheless   B. therefore   C. furthermore   D. meanwhile

10. The history of oil well drilling in the United States begins around the mid-1800s, almost at the <u>inception</u> of the Industrial Revolution.

    A. interval   B. beginning   C. presence   D. direction

B. Choose the one from the four choices that best completes the sentence.

1. Choice and voice may work in opposite directions; or they may _____ each other for a subset of consumers.

    A. compromise   B. complicate   C. comprehend   D. complement

2. I had had an _____ personality with a lot of friends, but when I lost the weight and grew so tall, I withdrew within myself.

    A. introverted   B. extroverted   C. internalized   D. externalized

3. However, they are extremely _____ and sensitive toward the feelings of others, and can be generous with their love.

    A. intuitive   B. deductive   C. distinctive   D. instinctive

4. A psychologist who _____ the effects of childbearing on women's body image will present her findings at the annual conference.

    A. improvised   B. implemented   C. investigated   D. invigorated

5. This video game is perfect for kids who like to experiment, _____ with stuff and design their own play worlds.

    A. tinker   B. tingle   C. timber   D. tinkle

6. China is home to a wide variety of different dialects. Many Chinese dialects have many differences and are usually mutually _____.

    A. intangible   B. unintelligible   C. intelligible   D. unintelligent

7. After the couple _____ a plan, they ordered a kit and hired a professional builder to lay the foundation and put up the materials from the package.

    A. called on   B. remarked on   C. settled on   D. reflected on

8. She has never _____ since becoming a Police Inspector because her work is both challenging and satisfying.

    A. looked through   B. looked back   C. looked down   D. looked up

9. The minimum wage is so low that often people working full-time on it still need welfare support to make ends _____.

A. meet   B. join   C. turn   D. cross

10. An author has had the rights to his latest book _____ by a Hollywood film company—before it has even been published.

    A. trapped up   B. skipped up   C. slapped up   D. snapped up

C. Complete each sentence with the proper form of the word given in the parenthesis.

1. This multi-part TV series addresses the fundamental and innate human nature of _____ and our inherent fascination with the world. (curious)

2. He is in the full _____ that real knowledge is the end product of a thorough study of the history. (convince)

3. US immigration policy should give _____ to people with education and experience in innovative technologies. (prior)

4. The question of what factors cause the formation and _____ of trends is an important one that has not been answered yet. (persist)

5. A researcher should obtain a certificate when he or she collects information from or about subjects that is _____ and sensitive. (identify)

6. Google has notified Federal regulators that it is forming an energy _____ that would buy and sell power on the wholesale market. (subsidy)

7. She thought her life was over, but imagine her _____ when she discovered that the fish was enchanted. (amaze)

8. It is each customer's responsibility to follow the hardware _____ listed below when purchasing their own hardware. (specific)

9. The company works around the globe and around the clock, offering _____ solutions to design needs in virtually every manufacturing arena. (innovate)

10. One way to get some good insights into what works and what doesn't is to see what your _____ are up to. (compete)

Part III   Cloze

Directions: There are totally 15 blanks in the following passage. Fill each blank with one word only.

If you were to begin a new job tomorrow, you would bring with you some basic strengths and weaknesses. Success or failure in your work would depend, to a great __1__, on your ability to use your strengths and weaknesses to the best __2__. Of the utmost importance is your attitude. A person who begins a job __3__ that he isn't going to like it or is sure that he is going to ail is exhibiting a weakness which can only hinder his success. __4__, a person who is secure in his belief that he is probably as __5__ of doing the work as anyone else and who is willing to make a cheerful __6__ at it possesses a certain strength of purpose. The chances are that he will do well. Having the __7__ skills for a particular job is strength. Lacking those skills is __8__ a weakness.

This book has been designed to help you __9__ on the strength and overcome the __10__ that you bring to the job of learning. But in groups to measure your development, you must first ___11___ stock of somewhere you stand now. As we get further along in the book, we'll be ___12___ in some detail with specific processes for developing and strengthening learning skills. ___13___, to begin with, you should pause to examine your present strengths and weaknesses in three areas that are ___14___ to your success or failure in school: your ___15___, your reading and communication skills, and your study habits.

1. A. measure   B. sense   C. extent   D. length
2. A. advantage   B. interest   C. purpose   D. point
3. A. convince   B. convinced   C. convincing   D. to convince
4. A. On the contrary B. In contrast   C. As a result   D. On the other hand
5. A. competent   B. qualified   C. capable   D. equitable
6. A. impact   B. length   C. effort   D. attempt
7. A. prerequisite   B. exquisite   C. expertise   D. prescriptive
8. A. ostensibly   B. apparently   C. obviously   D. seemingly
9. A. insist   B. retain   C. utilize   D. capitalize
10. A. idea   B. weakness   C. strength   D. advantage
11. A. make   B. take   C. do   D. give
12. A. handling   B. resolving   C. providing   D. dealing
13. A. Moreover   B. However   C. Therefore   D. Furthermore
14. A. critical   B. indispensable C. inseparable   D. necessary
15. A. intelligence B. work   C. attitude   D. weakness

Part IV Writing

Directions:Develop each of the following topics into an essay of about 200 words.

1. Opportunity and Success
2. Is Failure a Bad Thing?
3. Nothing succeeds like success. Interpret your understanding of the proverb.

Section B Extensive Reading and Translation

My Way to Success

By Wang An

[1] I find it somewhat surprising that so many talented people derail themselves one way or another during their lives. People fail to accomplish what they set out to do, or if they do accomplish something, all too often a meteoric rise triggers a precipitous fall. Of course, there is a strong element of luck in both success and failure, but it is my belief that there are no "secrets" to success. People fail for the most part because they shoot themselves in the foot. If you go for a long time without shooting yourself in the foot, other people start calling you a genius. But if there is anything that compelled me to write this book, it is to show that success is more a function of consistent common sense than of genius.

[2] I came to this country forty-one years ago from China. During the years since, America and American business have passed through several transformations,

including the emergence of the United States as the world leader in high technology following World War II. I have played a small role in this era. As a researcher at the Harvard Computation Laboratory in the late 1940s, I helped develop magnetic memory cores, which were essential to the development of modern computers. Later I became a businessman seeking to find and market applications of my innovations in digital electronics.

[3] In the thirty-five years since I founded Wang Laboratories, the company has grown from a one-man shop to an almost three-billion multinational company that employs over thirty thousand people. It has also changed from a company that produced specialized digital equipment for government, scientific laboratories, and industry into a company whose products bring the power of computers into every corner of the office. Throughout these transitions, the company has continued to grow at an average compounded rate of 42 percent.

[4] Over the years, the financial community came to take this kind of growth for granted, and the company has often been singled out as an exemplar of long-term planning. However, as anyone in business knows, earnings growth can never be taken for granted, over the long term, the medium term, or the shout term. (1) As markets change and a company grows, it must adapt, and the transitions necessary for adaptation are not always smooth, even if from a distance growth looks smooth

and continuous.

[5] When I founded the company, I never expected that it would grow to its present size. Nor did I look thirty-five years down the road and foresee the unfolding of the computer era. I knew that it would be foolhardy to attempt to predict the distant future. Progress does not follow a straight line; the future is not mere projection of trends in the present. Rather, it is revolutionary (which is why we speak of the computer revolution). It overturns the conventional wisdom of the present, which often conceals or ignores the clues to the future. In the late 1940s, when I was doing my research on magnetic core memory, the conventional wisdom was that a few large computers might satisfy all imaginable computer needs. While this may seem amusing and shortsighted from the vantage point of the present, it reflected the views of such eminent people as computer pioneer Howard Aiken, who looked at society and the economy and came to what they believed was sensible conclusion.

[6] While the computer revolution has produced an enormous industry, few of its commercial pioneers shared in this success. At any given moment in this revolution, the future was shrouded in uncertainty. (2) A number of pioneers made the humbling discovery that technological wizardry did not necessarily translate into an understanding of markets and society—and the way both change. Technology does not stand apart from society; each is constantly affecting the shape of the other.

[7] Given this revolutionary nature of the future, I have come to see that the key to long-term survival for a company is adaptability. One can sense change even if one doesn't know where it will ultimately lead. This does not mean looking decades into the future, but instead taking a clear-eyed look at the present and anticipating human needs in three or perhaps five years.

[8] Because in technology I have always been driven by society's needs, I have been able to adapt. In technology, this means delivering solutions rather than computers. Just as an automobile dealer does not ask a customer to study automotive engineering, a computer firm should not demand that its customers learn about computers. Most people do not want to study computer science any more than a commuter wants to study the internal combustion engine. On the other hand, if a machine makes their work more efficient and less of a chore, they will be interested, and they will not really care whether or not the machine is called a computer.

[9] (3) At various points in my company's history, we have been will positioned both to discover and to take advantage of opportunities as they arose. This is to some degree the result of luck, but it is also the result of the decisions I made at every stage of our growth-about technology, products, management, and finance. Because I had no formal training in any of these fields with the exception of engineering, I had to learn to meet each challenge of managing a business as it arose.

[10] My approach to management has been quite simple. At each stage of the growth of Wang Laboratories, I acquired the knowledge necessary to manage the next stage of growth. To grow faster than that, or to undertake projects that you are not yet prepared for, is to court disaster. I never really wanted Wang Laboratories to grow faster than 50 percent annually, because in any given year, I felt that I could only learn to manage a company 50 percent larger than the one I was then managing. With each small challenge I met, I was better prepared and more confident about my ability to meet a slightly greater challenge during the next phase of growth.

[11] Today I have the luxury of looking back and analyzing what lay behind this approach. One

thing I have discovered is that attitudes and values that I acquire in China long before I came to the United States have had a great bearing on the way I do business. These values have much in common with some of the virtues of Confucianism, the system of Chinese thought that stresses proper behavior and moderation. However, although I respect the spirit of Confucianism, I have not tried to adapt this ancient Chinese philosophy to modern America. I have not tried to devise a system at all.

[12] Behind my decision-making process there lie certain attributes or virtues which I believe play a role in the success or failure of a business. Perhaps the most important of these is simplicity. I am not fan of convoluted arguments or explanations. (4) No matter how intricate a technological or scientific problem is, it can usually be reduced to a simple, comprehensible form. In my own specialty, electronics, the simplest solution is usually the best solution.

[13] In the same way, even though a problem facing a businessman might seem incredibly complex and involve many variables, usually, upon contemplation, it will resolve into a simpler form and the key variable will emerge. In 1971, when I decided that we had to get out of the electronic calculator business, everybody around me was concerned with such things as market share, maintaining our competitive position, and our revenue stream. I was focused on the strategic implications of plummeting prices as semiconductor integrated circuits made their presence felt. Quite simply, I could see that calculators were becoming a commodity in the sense that people could now shop among brands on the basis of price rather than performance. I felt that we were not the best-positioned firm to compete in a commodity market. While the decision was not obvious, it was simple once one looked past the clutter.

[14] Besides simplicity, other things I have found to be essential to success are communication, moderation and patience, adaptability, decisiveness, confidence, unconventional thinking, social responsibility, and last, but by no means least, luck. (5) The importance of these attributes is in their interaction. Some of them are antithetical to others—patience will often collide with decisiveness, for instance—and yet it is hard to think of any of my decisions in which they did not play a role.

[15] If any one concept emerges from the interplay of these traits, it is that of balance—very much a Confucian ideal. Balance is really nothing more than an orientation that gives you a sense of where you are in any given situation. It is what prevents you from getting so caught up in the pressures of the moment that you lose sight of where you are going and what must be done. It is what tempers decisiveness so that it does not lead to dictatorship. It is what tempers confidence so that a useful trait does not become a dangerous one.

[16] Perhaps the hardest thing for an aggressive person to learn is to rein his instincts in the interests of long-term success. I did not found a computer company in 1951. The huge expense of such an enterprise made it an impractical idea. It was not until nearly two decades later that the company had evolved to the point where designing and building a computer was a logical thing for Wang Laboratories to do. By then we had the resources, the marketing skills and the stability to embark on an undertaking of this scale.

[17] Today the high-tech marketplace is an intensely competitive arena, I and a number of entrepreneurs who left the shelter of major corporations or academia to set out on their own have

discovered that it is not enough to have a good idea, or even a good product, in order to start a corporation that will survive amid the giants of domestic and foreign competition. This has produced a counterreaction of sorts, in which once again people are beginning to argue that without specialized expertise in marketing, management, and finance as well as technological prowess, the lone amateur can not make it.

[18] I do not think this is so. Surely the situation today poses no greater challenges than I faced when I started a business as a recent immigrant to this country. Change itself continually creates opportunities for those who recognize its importance, whether they are inside or outside the establishment. One does not have to be a specialist to succeed, and perhaps more important, one does not have to come from a particular class or ethnic group or political party. I discovered that with some common sense and discipline, I could compete and succeed in what was at first an alien society. I discovered that I could do this without leaving my values behind me when I went to work in the morning. I certainly made mistakes along the way, but even then, I found that I could minimize their consequences and turn them into lessons from which something positive might come.

[19] I offer readers of this book the proposition that there is no magic in mastering the challenges of starting and nurturing a business, even in an arena as esoteric as high technology. One can succeed without being possessed of prophetic powers. One can prosper without getting an MBA, or being bullied by MBAs, or succumbing to the management fads that periodically capture the attention of America's boardrooms. I also believe that the approach to business I am describing might benefit people in any number of occupations. I hope therefore that these pages will not be read as a catalog of my achievements but rather as a case study of one man making decisions and taking risks. The landscape of society and business has changed since I started out, and it will continue to change, but the opportunities remain for those who choose to seize them.

Part A Translate English into Chinese

I. Translate the underlined sentences in the above text into Chinese.

II. Translate paragraphs 1, 17 and 18 in the above text into Chinese.

Part B Translate Chinese into English

I. Translate the following sentences into English with the words or phrases in the passage in Section B.

1. 经过 30 年的改革开放,中国成功实现了从高度集中的计划经济体制到充满活力的社会主义市场经济体制的伟大历史转折。

2. 这学期我们都学习得不错,我真不明白为什么我们老师单单只表扬了班长一个人。

3. 可以这样说:"公司是一种人为的存在,看不见,摸不着,仅仅存在于法律的考虑之中"。

4. 整个社会将走上生产发展、生活富足、生态良好的文明发展道路。

5. 如果说商人们不惜花本钱做广告的话,那一定是因为他们知道人们容易接受新闻媒介所提供的劝告。

II. Translate the following paragraph into English.

今天在美国生活着几百万华人,他们的祖先大多数来自中国的东南部。这些地区在当时还算是中国较发达的地区,可他们中的许多人从未受过学校教育。尽管这些美籍华人已离开故土数十年,但仍然保持着中国古老文化的诸多特色,如:他们的家庭纽带依然十分牢固,家庭成员之间在精神上相互支持,必要的时候在经济上也相互帮助。他们为继承和发扬中华民族重视教育、努力工作、谋求发展等美德而感到骄傲。正是这些优良传统使他们的后代中许多人成为非常成功的医生、律师及其他专业人员。

Unit 7

Section A   Intensive Reading and Writing

What the Hidden Persuaders
Are up to Nowadays

[1] People keep asking me what the hidden persuaders are up to nowadays. So, for a few months, I revisited the persuasion specialists. The demographers and motivational researchers, I found, are still very much with us, but admen (= ad-men) today are also listening to other kinds of behavior specialists. It's a less irrational world than 20 years ago perhaps, but more unpredictable.

[2] Admen seek trustworthy predictions on how we the consumers are going to react to their efforts. Years ago they learned that we may lie politely when discussing ads or products, so, increasingly, the advertising world has turned to our bodies for clues to our real feelings.

[3] Take our eyes. There is one computerized machine that tracks their movement as they examine a printed ad. This spots the elements in the ad that have the most "stopping power". For overall reactions to an ad or commercial, some admen have been trying the pupillometer, a machine that measures the pupil under stimulation.

[4] The pupil expands when there is arousal of interest, although this can lead to mistaken conclusions. A marketer of frozen fried potatoes was pleased by reports of significant expansion during its TV ad. But further analysis indicated that it was the sizzling steak in the ad, not the fried potatoes, that was causing the expansion. What's more, the pupillometer cannot tell whether a viewer likes or dislikes an ad. (We are also aroused by ads that annoy us.) This caused some of its users to become dissatisfied, but others stick with it as at least helpful. Arousal is something. Without it the admen are inevitably wasting money.

[5] There are also machines that offer voice-pitch analysis. First, our normal voices are taped

and then our voices while commenting on an ad or product. A computer reports whether we are offering lip service, a polite lie or a firm opinion.

[6] In the testing of two commercials with children in them, other kids' comments seemed about equally approving. The mechanical detective, however, reported that one of the commercials simply interested the kids, whereas the other packed an emotional impact that they found hard to express.

[7] Viewing rooms are used to try out commercials and programs on off-the-street people. Viewers push buttons to indicate how interested or bored they are.

[8] One technique for gauging ad impact is to measure brain waves with electrodes. If a person is really interested in something, his brain emits fast beta waves. If he is in a passive, relaxed state, his brain emits the much slower alpha waves. An airline has used brainwave testing to choose its commercial spokesman. Networks have used the test to check out actors and specific scenes in pilot films that need a sponsor.

[9] Admen also seek to sharpen their word power to move us to action. Some have turned to psycholinguistics—the deepdown meaning of words—and to a specialty called psychographic segmentation.

[10] A few years ago Colgate-Palmolive[1] was eager to launch a new soap. Now, for most people, the promise of cleanliness ranks low as a compelling reason for buying soap. It's assumed. So soap makers promise not only cleanliness but one of two instinctive appeals—physical attractiveness (a turning up of complexion) or a deodorant (a pleasant smell).

[11] Colgate-Palmolive turned to psychographic segmentation to find a position within the "deodorant" end of the soap field. The segmenters found a psychological type they called independents—the ambitious, forceful, self-assured types with a positive outlook on life, mainly men, who like to take cold showers.

[12] Their big need, over and above cleanliness, was a sense of refreshment. What kind of imagery could offer refreshment? Colgate researchers thought of spring of greenery and that led them to think of Ireland, which has a nationally advertised image picturing cool, misty, outdoor greenery.

[13] So the Colgate people hired a rugged, self-assured male with a bit of Irish accent as a spokesman and concocted a soap with green and white lines. The bar was packaged in a manly green-against-black wrapper (the black had come out of psychological research), and they hailed it as Irish spring—now a big success in the soap field.

[14] Advertising people have long been worried about not being able to say much in a 15- or 30-second commercial. So they experimented with faster talking. Typically, when you run a recorded message at speeds significantly faster than normal you get Donald Duck quackery. But psychologists working with electronic specialists came up with a computerized time compression device that creates a normal sounding voice even when the recording is speeded up by 40 percent. Research has also indicated that listeners actually preferred messages at faster-than-normal speed and remembered them better.

[15] Meanwhile, at one of the world's largest advertising agencies, J. Walter Thompson[2], technicians forecast that many TV messages will be coming at us in three-second bursts, combining words, symbols and other imagery. The messages will be almost subliminal.

[16] The subliminal approach is to get messages to us beneath our level of awareness. It can be a voice too low for us to hear consciously. It can be a message flashed on a screen too rapidly for us to notice, or a filmed message shown continuously but dimly.

[17] Subliminal seduction has been banned by most broadcasters, but nothing prevents its use in stores, movies and salesrooms. Several dozen department stores use it to reduce shoplifting.

[18] Such messages as "I am honest, I will not steal" are mixed with background music and continually repeated. One East Coast retail chain reported a one-third drop in theft in a nine-month period.

[19] The sale of imagery and symbols continues to fascinate admen. In one experiment, 200 women were questioned, ostensibly about color schemes in furniture design. For their co-operation the women were given a supply of cold cream. They were to take home and try out two samples. When they came back for their next advice-giving session, they would be given an ample supply of the cold cream of their choice.

[20] Both sample jars were labeled "high-quality cold cream". The cap of one jar had a design with two triangles on it. The cap of the other jar had two circles. The cold cream inside the jars was identical, yet 80 percent of the women asked for the one with the circle design on the cap. They liked the consistency of that cream better. They found it easier to apply and definitely of finer quality. All because, it seems, women prefer circles to triangles.

[21] Today, as when I first reported on persuasion techniques in advertising, our hidden needs are still very much on admen's minds. One need that has grown greatly in two decades—perhaps because of all the moving and the breaking up of families—is warm human contact.

[22] The American Telephone and Telegram Company[3] used this need to generate more long-distance calls. Historically, such calls were associated with accidents, death in the family and other stressful situations. AT&T wanted long-distance calling to become casual spur-of-the-moment fun. Hence the jingle, "reach out, reach out and touch someone", played against various scenes filled with good friendship.

[23] Then there was a manufacturer of hay balers who sought more farmers to buy his machine. Psychologist Ernest Dichter[4], an old master at persuasion, came up with a technique based on the theory that instant reward is better in creating a sense of achievement than long-delayed reward—in this case a check for the hay baler two months later.

[24] Dichter recommended attaching a rear-view mirror and a bell to the baler. Every time a bundle of hay was assembled as the machine moved across a hayfield, the farmer could see it in the mirror. And when the bale dropped onto the field the bell rang. Thus the reward was not only instant but visual and audible. Farmers loved it. And so did the manufacturer, who started ringing up the hay-baler sales.

Notes to the Text

1. **Colgate-Palmolive**—an American diversified multinational corporation focused on the production, distribution and provision of household, health care and personal products, such as soaps,

detergents, and oral hygiene products (including toothpaste and toothbrushes). Under its "Hill's" brand, it is also a manufacturer of veterinary products. The company's corporate offices are on Park Avenue in Midtown Manhattan, New York City.

2. **J. Walter Thompson**—one of the largest advertising agencies in the United States and the fourth-biggest in the world. It is one of the key companies of Sir Martin Sorrell's WPP Group and is headquartered in New York.

   James Walter Thompson (1847—1928) was the namesake of the JWT advertising agency and a pioneer of many advertising techniques.

3. **The American Telephone and Telegram Company** (AT&T)—the largest provider of fixed telephony in the United States, and is also a provider of broadband and subscription television services. The company is headquartered in downtown Dallas, Texas.

4. **Ernest Dichter** (1907—1991)—an American-based psychologist and marketing expert who is often considered to be the "father of motivational research". Dichter is credited with originating the Exxon slogan "Put a tiger in your tank" in collaboration with Chicago advertising copywriter Frederick D. ("Sandy") Sulcer.

Part I Comprehension of the Text

1. Why are admen today also listening to other kinds of behavior specialists?
2. How can admen know what the consumers think of their ads?
3. What is subliminal approach?
4. According to the author, what are admen up to nowadays?
5. What is the author's purpose of writing this passage?

Part II Vocabulary

A. Choose the one from the four choices that best explains the underlined word or phrase.

1. The proposed legislation pays a lip service to the appointment of medically responsible physician with little authority over the final outcome.
   A. an empty compliment　　　　B. a white lie
   C. a fair comment　　　　　　D. support in words

2. This comes mostly from illegal drug trafficking, but also from ostensibly legal businesses such as construction, restaurants and supermarkets.
   A. seemingly　　B. purposely　　C. definitely　　D. seriously

3. Hawking radiation is an explanation of how radiation can be emitted from a black hole, despite its attractive power, due to quantum effects.
   A. checked out　　B. turned out　　C. given out　　D. put out

4. There are many other technologies that can be and are used to generate electricity such as solar photovoltaics and geothermal power.

A. produce   B. consume   C. manipulate   D. capture

5. Metabolism gets blamed when people put on weight or have trouble losing weight, but you can learn how to <u>speed up</u> your metabolism.

A. hinder   B. quicken   C. improve   D. ensure

6. People who make <u>irrational</u> decisions when faced with problems are at the mercy of their emotions, a study says.

A. unreasonable   B. insensitive   C. inappropriate   D. indefinite

7. An increasing number of machines are equipped with hardware that can be used to support <u>trustworthy</u> computing.

A. honest   B. conscientious   C. reliable   D. responsible

8. Any man who has once proclaimed violence as his method is <u>inevitably</u> forced to take the lie as his principle.

A. unavoidably   B. unbelievably   C. inexorably   D. irresistibly

9. The U. S. Forest Service has <u>banned</u> campfires in the wilderness area, including those fueled by charcoal.

A. opposed   B. approved   C. controlled   D. forbidden

10. If they can, chances are they will <u>comment on</u> it and that might influence the drawer, which would not be in the spirit of the game.

A. refer to   B. remark on   C. resort to   D. reflect on

B. Choose the one from the four choices that best completes the sentence.

1. We hope you take the opportunity to _____ the new site and give us some feedback on how you like it.

A. try on   B. try up   C. try out   D. try after

2. Against this background, experts at the Yale School of Public Health have _____ ten guiding principles to strengthen global health.

A. come up against   B. come up with   C. come up to   D. come up for

3. The untimely loss of her funny, kind hearted son is the last thing _____ when she goes to bed and the first thing she thinks about when she awakens.

A. in her mind   B. to her mind   C. out of her mind   D. on her mind

4. There are many foods including vegetables and fruits which can help to improve the _____ of your skin.

A. compensation   B. complexion   C. complication   D. composition

5. He moved in with the victim and her children after their relationship began, but was left homeless after they _____.

A. broke up   B. broke down   C. broke off   D. broke out

6. FDA strengthens inspecting the _____ between the information on labels of packages of products on the market and the contents of the products.

A. constituency   B. consistency   C. consultancy   D. constancy

7. The clerk in the checkout line _____ the purchases and then turned the display on the cash register so we could read the tally.

    A. rang out   B. rang in   C. rang up   D. rang down

8. She doesn't know her name, and the only _____ to her identity is a book of fairy tales tucked inside a white suitcase.

    A. evidence   B. clue   C. indication   D. proof

9. His pride and vanity _____ him to a form of government which favors his pretensions and gives him a share in its honors and distinctions.

    A. attach   B. attract   C. detach   D. deprive

10. Like many controversial films it has left critics divided; whilst many regard the film as depraved and disgusting others have _____ it as a masterpiece.

    A. deputed   B. referred   C. decried   D. hailed

C. Complete each sentence with the proper form of the word given in the parenthesis.

1. The mobile phone will soon become the most powerful channel for _____, more influential than TV, radio, print, or the Internet. (persuade)

2. With the _____ fierce competition, more and more people are bearing great pressure from study, work and life. (increase)

3. The trains in yesterday's crash were supposed to be in automatic operation, which means the operators would have been relying on the _____ system to run the trains. (computer)

4. Consumers can look at the ingredient label to determine if a _____ or antiperspirant contains parabens. (odor)

5. On summer days, the dazzling sunlight is often potent, but because the humidity is low, you can feel _____ of body and mind. (fresh)

6. Not so popular now due to competition, improved marketing research capabilities, and total production and marketing costs can be reduced by _____. (segment)

7. It is argued that globalization as a concept refers both to the _____ of the world and the intensification of consciousness of the world as a whole. (compress)

8. As well as wasting huge amounts of water, the noise of a _____ running toilet is enough to drive anyone mad. (continue)

9. The entire strategy of _____ is to bring things to state of pure appearance, to make them radiate and wear themselves out in the game of appearances. (seduce)

10. As a guest speaker, Jody has been presenting her _____ speeches around the world for over 13 years. (motive)

Part III Cloze

Directions: There are totally 15 blanks in the following passage. Fill each blank with one word only.

    A manufacturer does not usually deal directly with the people who use his products. He sells his products to them indirectly through __1__ outlets. Therefore his selling problem has two aspects: he must __2__ storekeepers that it will be __3__ for them to stock the things he manufactures, and he must __4__ thousands or millions of unseen people to buy his products from storekeepers in various places. This kind of selling __5__ both trade advertising and consumer advertising. The manufacturer places advertisements in trade magazines that are read by __6__ who sell his type of product. He then undertakes more costly advertising to __7__ the consumer.

Advertisers know from practical experience that products, old or new, cannot be __8__ people. In the modern economy "the consumer is the king". Customers are __9__ what they want. Much money is spent on research __10__ an effort to understand the consumer's desires. __11__ these efforts to please the public, __12__ are often fickle. They __13__ their preferences from one brand to another or from one type of product to another. In many instances no amount of advertising, __14__ clever or persuasive, can keep people from making such changes. __15__, advertising itself is often the cause of the customer's decision to change products.

1. A. wholesale   B. retail   C. wholesome   D. retailing

2. A. convince   B. advice   C. inform   D. prompt

3. A. triumphant   B. mandatory   C. profitable   D. privileged

4. A. advertise   B. induce   C. authorize   D. enlighten

5. A. calls on   B. calls off   C. calls up   D. calls for

6. A. retailers   B. consumers   C. merchants   D. readers

7. A. adapt to   B. appeal to   C. respond to   D. object to

8. A. forced on   B. promoted to   C. compelled by   D. coerced to

9. A. free of buying   B. free from buying   C. free with buying   D. free to buy

10. A. for   B. with   C. in   D. at

11. A. With regard to   B. In spite of   C. As a result of   D. In relation to

12. A. customers   B. manufacturers   C. advertisers   D. storekeepers

13. A. transfer   B. switch   C. transmit   D. exchange

14. A. if   B. though   C. however   D. while

15. A. In other words   B. Otherwise   C. As a result   D. On the other hand

Part IV   Writing

Directions: Develop each of the following topics into an essay of about 200 words.

1. Ads and Human Life

2. Advertisements on TV

3. Advantages of Ad

Section B　Extensive Reading and Translation

Marketing to Your Mind

By Alice Park

[1] Are you a Coke or Pepsi drinker? Do you pull into McDonald's golden arches or prefer to "have it your way" at Burger King? When it comes to toothpaste, which flavor gets you brushing, Colgate or Crest? (1) If you think it's just your taste buds that guide these preferences, you may be surprised by what neuroscientists are discovering when they peer inside the brain as it makes everyday choices like these.

[2] Don't worry—no one's scanning your head as you stand in front of the

beverage aisle or sit in line at the drive-through. Instead, brain scientists are asking volunteers to ponder purchasing choices while lying inside high-tech brain scanners. The resulting real-time images indicate where and how the brain analyzes options, weighs risks and rewards, factors in experiences and emotions and ultimately sets a preference. "We can use brain imaging to gain insight into the mechanisms behind people's decisions in a way that is often difficult to get at simply by asking a person or watching their behavior", says Dr. Gregory Berns, a psychiatrist at Emory University.

[3] To scientists, it's all part of the larger question of how the human brain makes decisions. But the answers may be invaluable to Big Business, which plowed an estimated $ 8 billion in 2006 into market research in an effort to predict—and sway—how we would spend our money. (2) In the past, marketers relied on relatively crude measures of what got us buying: focus-group questionnaires and measurements of eye movements and perspiration patterns (the more excited you get about something, the more you tend to sweat). Now researchers can go straight to the decider in chief—the brain itself, opening the door to a controversial new field dubbed neuromarketing.

[4] For now, most of the research is purely academic, although even brain experts anticipate that it's just a matter of time before their findings become a routine part of any smart corporation's marketing plans. Some lessons, particularly about how the brain interprets brand names, are already enticing advertisers. Take, for example, the classic taste test. P. Read Montague of Baylor College of Medicine performed his version of the Pepsi Challenge inside a functional magnetic resonance imaging (fMRI) machine in 2004. Montague gave 67 people a blind taste test of both Coke and Pepsi, then placed his subjects in the scanner, whose magnetic field measures how active cells are by recording

how much oxygen they consume for energy. (3) After tasting each drink, all the volunteers showed strong activation of the reward areas of the brain—which are associated with pleasure and satisfaction—and they were almost evenly split in their preferences for the two brands. But when Montague repeated the test and told them what they were drinking, three out of four people said they preferred Coke, and their brains showed why: not only were the reward systems active, but memory regions in the medial prefrontal cortex and hippocampus also lit up. "This showed that the brand alone has value in the brain system above and beyond the desire for the content of the can", says Montague. In other words, all those happy, energetic and glamorous people drinking Coke in commercials did exactly what they were supposed to do: seeped into the brain and left associations so powerful they could even override a preference for the taste of Pepsi.

[5] Stanford neuroscientist Brian Knutson has zeroed in on a more primitive aspect of making choices. "We come equipped to assess potentially good things and potentially bad things", he says. "There should be stuff in your brain that promotes your survival, whether you have learned those things or not—such as being scared of the dark or the unknown." (4) Knutson calls these anticipatory emotions, and he believes that even before the cognitive areas of the brain are brought in to assess options, these more intuitive and emotional regions are already priming the decision-making process and can foreshadow the outcome. Such primitive triggers almost certainly afforded survival advantages to our ancestors when they decided which plants to pick or which caves to enter, but Knutson surmises that vestiges of this system are at work as we make more mundane choices at the mall. There, it's the match between the value of a product and its price that triggers an anticipation of pleasure or pain.

[6] To test his theory, Knutson and his team devised a way to mimic these same intuitive reactions in the lab. He gave subjects $ 20 each and, while they were in the fMRI machine, presented them with pictures of 80 products, each followed by a price. Subjects then had the option of purchasing each item on display. As they viewed products they preferred, Knutson saw activity in the nucleus accumbens, a region of the brain involved in anticipating pleasant outcomes. If, on the other hand, the subjects thought the price of these items was too high, there was increased activity in the insula—an area involved in anticipating pain. (5) "The idea is that if you can look into people's brains right before they make certain decisions, you can get a handle on these two feelings and do a better job of predicting what they are about to do", Knutson says. "I believe anticipatory emotions not only bias but drive decision making."

[7] All of this, of course, is whirring along at the brain's split-second pace, and as imaging technology improves, Knutson is hopeful that he and others will be able to see in even more detail the circuits in the brain activated during a decision. Already, according to Montague, these images have revealed surprising things about how the brain pares down the decision-making process by setting up shortcuts to make its analysis more efficient. To save time, the brain doesn't run through the laundry list of risks, benefits and value judgments each time. Whenever it can, it relies on a type of "quick key" that takes advantage of experiences and stored information. That's where things like brands, familiarity and trust come in—they're a shortcut for knowing what to expect. "You run from the devil you know", says Montague. "And you run to the brand that you know, because to sit there and

deliberate chews up time, and that makes you less efficient than the next guy."

[8] That's certainly music to advertisers' ears, but, warn neuroscientists, it's unlikely that our purchasing behavior follows a single pathway. Montague, for one, is investigating how factors like trust, altruism and the feeling of obligation when someone does you a favor can divert and modify steps in the decision-making tree. "The capacity to use brain responses and relate them to behavior has accelerated at a breathtaking pace over the past four years and yielded an incredible amount of information", he says. How marketers use that data to hone their messages remains to be seen.

Part A   Translate English into Chinese

I. Translate the underlined sentences in the above text into Chinese.

II. Translate paragraphs 7 and 8 in the above text into Chinese.

Part B   Translate Chinese into English

I. Translate the following sentences into English with the words or phrases in the passage in Section B.

1. 即使总统否决了这个法案,国会可以通过参众两院 2/3 的多数票来推翻总统的否决。
2. 老师打开门,让小孩看着架子上那些玩具,试图吸引他走进教室。
3. 经过一周的调查走访,警方将注意力集中在了三天前来到本市的两个可疑分子身上。
4. 他们推测是因为低估了服务领域的通胀,因此实际增长才会被高估。
5. 对于腐败行为和成功破获腐败犯罪的经常性报道能够对所有的玩家形成压力,促使他们停止滥用职权。

II. Translate the following paragraph into English.

为了更好地了解广告商是如何说服我们去买他们的产品的,我们最好全面分析一下人的本性。广告商多年前就已发现人都喜欢白拿东西。因此用免费这个迷人的字眼作为广告的开头很少会失败。广告商不但免费提供样品,还免费提供汽车、住房和环球旅行。电台和电视台使得广告商用这种方法来吸引千百万人的注意成为了可能。

Unit 8

Section A Intensive Reading and Writing

What is Science?

By George Orwell[1]

[1] In last week's *Tribune*[2], there was an interesting letter from Mr. J. Stewart Cook, in which he suggested that the best way of avoiding the danger of a 'scientific hierarchy' would be to see to it that every member of the general public was, as far as possible, scientifically educated. At the same time, scientists should be brought out of their isolation and encouraged to take a greater part in politics and administration.

[2] As a general statement, I think most of us would agree with this, but I notice that, as usual, Mr. Cook does not define science, and merely implies in passing that it means certain exact sciences whose experiments can be made under laboratory conditions. Thus, adult education tends "to neglect scientific studies in favour of literary, economic and social subjects", economics and sociology not being regarded as branches of science. Apparently, this point is of great importance. For the word science is at present used in at least two meanings, and the whole question of scientific education is obscured by the current tendency to dodge from one meaning to the other.

[3] Science is generally taken as meaning either (a) the exact sciences, such as chemistry, physics, etc., or (b) a method of thought which obtains verifiable results by reasoning logically from observed fact.

[4] If you ask any scientist, or indeed almost any educated person, "What is science?" you are likely to get an answer approximating to (b). In everyday life, however, both in speaking and in writing, when people say "science" they mean (a). Science means something that happens in a laboratory: the very word calls up a picture of graphs, test-tubes, balances, Bunsen burners[3],

microscopes. A biologist, and astronomer, perhaps a psychologist or a mathematician is described as a "man of science": no one would think of applying this term to a statesman, a poet, a journalist or even a philosopher. And those who tell us that the young must be scientifically educated mean, almost invariably, that they should be taught more about radioactivity, or the stars, or the physiology or their own bodies, rather than that they should be taught to think more exactly.

[5] This confusion of meaning, which is partly deliberate, has in it a great danger. Implied in the demand for more scientific education is the claim that if one has been scientifically trained one's approach to *all* subjects will be more intelligent than if one had had no such training. A scientist's political opinions, it is assumed, his opinions on sociological questions, on morals, on philosophy, perhaps even on the arts, will be more valuable than those of a layman. The world, in other words, would be a better place if the scientists were in control of it. But a "scientist", as we have just seen, means in practice a specialist in one of the exact sciences. It follows that a chemist or a physicist, as such, is politically more intelligent than a poet or a lawyer, as such. And, in fact, there are already millions of people who do believe this.

[6] But is it really true that a "scientist", in this narrower sense, is any likelier than other people to approach non-scientific problems in an objective way? There is not much reason for thinking so. Take one simple test—the ability to withstand nationalism. It is often loosely said that "Science is international", but in practice the scientific workers of all countries line up behind their own governments with fewer scruples than are felt by the writers and the artists. The German scientific community, as a whole, made no resistance to Hitler. Hitler may have ruined the long-term prospects of German science, but there were still plenty of gifted men doing the necessary research on such things as synthetic oil, jet planes, rocket projectiles and the atomic bomb. Without them the German war machine could never have been built up.

[7] On the other hand, what happened to German literature when the Nazis came to power? I believe no exhaustive lists have been published, but I imagine that the number of German scientists— Jews apart—who voluntarily exiled themselves or were persecuted by the règime was much smaller than the number of writers and journalists. More sinister than this, a number of German scientists swallowed the monstrosity of "racial science". You can find some of the statements to which they set their names in Professor Brady's[4] *The Spirit and Structure of German Fascism*.

[8] But, in slightly different forms, it is the same picture everywhere. In England, a large proportion of our leading scientists accept the structure of capitalist society, as can be seen from the comparative freedom with which they are given knighthoods, baronetcies and even peerages. Since Tennyson[5], no English writer worth reading—one might, perhaps, make an exception of Sir Max Beerbohm[6]—has been given a title. ...The fact is that a mere training in one or more of the exact sciences, even combined with very high gifts, is no guarantee of a humane or sceptical outlook. The physicists of half a dozen great nations, all feverishly and secretly working away at the atomic bomb, are a demonstration of this.

[9] But does all this mean that the general public should *not* be more scientifically educated? On the contrary! All it means is that scientific education for the masses will do little good, and probably a lot of harm, if it simply boils down to more physics, more chemistry, more biology, etc. ,

to the detriment of literature and history. Its probable effect on the average human being would be to narrow the range of his thoughts and make him more than ever contemptuous of such knowledge as he did not possess: and his political reactions would probably be somewhat less intelligent than those of an illiterate peasant who retained a few historical memories and a fairly sound aesthetic sense.

[10] Clearly, scientific education ought to mean the implanting of a rational, sceptical, experimental habit of mind. It ought to mean acquiring a *method*—a method that can be used on any problem that one meets—and not simply piling up a lot of facts. Put it in those words, and the apologist of scientific education will usually agree. Press him further, ask him to particularize, and somehow it always turns out that scientific education means more attention to the sciences, in other words—more *facts*. The idea that science means a way of looking at the world, and not simply a body of knowledge, is in practice strongly resisted. I think sheer professional jealousy is part of the reason for this. For if science is simply a method or an attitude, so that anyone whose thought-processes are sufficiently rational can in some sense be described as a scientist—what then becomes of the enormous prestige now enjoyed by the chemist, the physicist, etc. and his claim to be somehow wiser than the rest of us?

[11] A hundred years ago, Charles Kingsley[7] described science as "making nasty smell in a laboratory". A year or two ago a young industrial chemist informed me, smugly, that he "could not see what the use of poetry was". So the pendulum swings to and fro, but it does not seem to me that one attitude is any better than the other. At the moment, science is on the upgrade, and so we hear, quite rightly, the claim that the masses should be scientifically educated: we do not hear, as we ought, the counter-claim that the scientists themselves would benefit by a little education. Just before writing this, I saw in an American magazine the statement that a number of British and American physicists refused from the start to do research on the atomic bomb, well knowing what use would be made of it. Here you have a group of same men in the middle of a world of lunatics. And though no names were published, I think it would be a safe guess that all of them were people with some kind of general cultural background, some acquaintance with history or literature or the arts—in short, people whose interests were not, in the current sense of the word, purely scientific.

Notes to the Text

1. **George Orwell** (25 June 1903—21 January 1950)—the pen name of **Eric Arthur Blair**, an English author and journalist. His work is marked by keen intelligence and wit, a profound awareness of social injustice, an intense, revolutionary opposition to totalitarianism, a passion for clarity in language and a belief in democratic socialism. Orwell wrote fiction, polemical journalism, literary criticism and poetry. He is best known for the dystopian novel *Nineteen Eighty-Four* (published in 1949) and the satirical novella *Animal Farm* (1945). They have together sold more copies than any two books by any other twentieth-century author. His *Homage to Catalonia* (1938), an account of his experiences as a volunteer on the Republican side during the Spanish Civil War, together with his numerous essays on politics, literature, language and culture, is widely acclaimed.

2. *Tribune*—a democratic socialist weekly set up in early 1937, currently a magazine though in past more often a newspaper, published in London. It considers itself "A thorn in the side of all governments, constructively to Labour, unforgiving to Conservatives".

3. **Bunsen burner**—named after Robert Bunsen, is a common piece of laboratory equipment that produces a single open gas flame, which is used for heating, sterilization, and combustion.

4. **Robert A. Brady** (1901—1963)—an American economist who analyzed the dynamics of technological change and the structure of business enterprise. Brady developed a potent analysis of fascism and other emerging authoritarian economic and cultural practices. His essential work is "about power and the organization of power around the logic of technology as operated under capitalism", yielding insights and understanding of modern society's careening path between enhancing or destroying "life and culture". In *The Spirit and Structure of German Fascism* (1937) and *Business as a System of Power* (1943), important works in historical and comparative economics, Brady traced the rise of bureaucratic centralism in Germany, France, Italy, Japan and the United States; and the emergence of an authoritarian model of economic growth and development.

5. **Alfred Tennyson** (1809—1892)—an English poet. The most famous poet of the Victorian age, he was a profound spokesman for the ideas and values of his times.

6. **Sir Max Beerbohm** (1872—1956)—English essayist, caricaturist, and parodist. He contributed to the famous Yellow Bookwhile still an undergraduate at Oxford. In 1898 he succeeded G. B. Shaw as drama critic for the Saturday Review. A charming, witty, and elegant man, Beerbohm was a brilliant parodist and the master of a polished prose style. Beerbohm was accomplished at drawing, and he published several volumes of excellent caricatures. He was knighted in 1939 on his return from Italy, where he had lived from 1910.

7. **Charles Kingsley** (1819—1875), English author and clergyman. From 1860 to 1869 he was professor of modern history at Cambridge and in 1873 was appointed canon of Westminster.

Part I Comprehension of the Text

1. What is the general understanding of SCIENCE? What is the author's definition of SCIENCE?
2. According to the author, what is Scientific Education? Is it important? Why?
3. What does the author try to illustrate with the examples of Germany and England?
4. What are the author's main points of view in this passage? To what extent do you agree with the author?
5. What's your understanding of the saying "Science is international"?

Part II Vocabulary

A. Choose the one from the four choices that best explains the underlined word or phrase.

1. Rankings and awards reflect the high international <u>prestige</u> enjoyed by the School of Social Sciences

institutes.

                     B. reputation   C. recognition   D. preference

                to dodge doing the job and when they couldn't get out if it, they did it with a

              an.

    A. unish   B. ignore   C. avoid   D. devoid

3. As the article implies in passing, this is probably going to become one more way that our educational system reinforces class differences.

   A. incidentally   B. accidentally   C. definitely   D. exclusively

4. Ordinary stresses of life, such as problems at work or in relationships, decrease the ability to withstand discomfort and pain.

   A. resist   B. assist   C. persist   D. insist

5. By taking deliberate actions with each step, people will pay attention to your schedule, have more respect and not demand you follow theirs.

   A. absolute   B. careful   C. resolute   D. purposeful

6. For centuries the castle with its pointed towers has had a sinister reputation for housing an unspeakable, terrible secret.

   A. ominous   B. dreadful   C. pious   D. woeful

7. He was criticized for making this move but he swallowed the criticism because he knew he'd done the right thing.

   A. believed   B. accepted   C. consumed   D. devoured

8. The retired generals and admirals who line up behind their preferred candidate don't want to dismantle the national security state.

   A. admired   B. applauded   C. supported   D. respected

9. As prices have dropped lower and lower, the outlook looks black for many companies in the city.

   A. prospect   B. perspective   C. perception   D. proportion

10. Every action at local level is equally vital for the continued economical and social development of the world without detriment to the environment.

   A. profit   B. benefit   C. scruple   D. damage

B. Choose the one from the four choices that best completes the sentence.

1. During recent years there has been a great debate about the clash of civilizations, which ultimately _____ a clash between religions.

   A. devolves into   B. dodges from   C. boils down to   D. becomes of

2. Sometimes when the conscious mind cannot resolve a problem the subconscious mind continues to _____ at it behind the scenes.

   A. work away   B. work out   C. work down   D. work through

3. Originally heated by multiple fireplaces, the building _____ the use of a few fireplaces in larger banquet rooms.

   A. attains   B. obtains   C. detains   D. retains

4. A further step taken in many practical applications is that the physical quantities across each entry region on the boundary are _____ to be uniform.

A. appreciated   B. approximated   C. apprehended   D. appropriated

5. He says that painting kept him sane in a world of _____ and made life in Iraq bearable and sometimes even pleasant.

A. maniacs   B. lunatics   C. idiots   D. refugees

6. As soon as it is _____ by selfish desires, even the mind of the great man will be divided and narrow like that of the small man.

A. crippled   B. deviated   C. obscured   D. penalized

7. It is not possible to frame a set of rules which will _____ all the duties of the lawyer in all the varied relations of his professional life.

A. characterize   B. dramatize   C. visualize   D. particularize

8. They do not _____ to tell lies to screen themselves when they commit a fault, and when detected, to pass off the lie with a jest.

A. scruple   B. cripple   C. disciple   D. crumple

9. Christians in Germany were _____ by Hitler, because their devotion to Christ exceeded their loyalty to the Nazi government.

A. persecuted   B. prosecuted   C. confiscated   D. eradicated

10. The term environmental science _____ a picture of scientists in white lab coats or decontamination suits, wearing gas masks and carrying instruments.

A. piles up   B. makes up   C. calls up   D. builds up

C. Complete each sentence with the proper form of the word given in the parenthesis.

1. A complex system that works is _____ found to have evolved from a simple system that worked. (vary)

2. He declared further that he never saw a man so humble in all things or so _____ of worldly glory and the things that accompany it. (contempt)

3. They are by no means _____ lists of everything available in the field, rather they are resources that are at hand and available for you to borrow. (exhaust)

4. Both collectors and decorators alike are searching _____ for customized and rare galleries and selections. (fever)

5. They thought that the problem of the aboriginals had arisen out of their _____ from the main body of the community. (isolate)

6. The government should have first launched efforts to remove _____ and educate people at the grassroots level. (literate)

7. He believed that a society that creates the _____ of war does not deserve art, so he decided to give it anti-art—not beauty but ugliness. (monster)

8. Philosophical questions have an intrinsic intellectual fascination, and some _____ with philosophy is an important part of a liberal education. (acquaint)

9. Love sees sharply, hatred sees even sharper, but _____ sees the sharpest for it is love and hate at the same time. (jealous)

10. Applicants must provide _____ proof of their household composition and size, including the age and disability status of each household member. (verify)

Part III　Error Correction

Directions: In the following passage, there is one error in each of the numbered sentences. Identify the error and then correct it in the space provided following the passage.

The most important starting point for improving the understanding of silence is undoubtedly an adequate scientific education at school. (1) Public attitudes towards science owe much the way science is taught in these institutions. (2) Today, school is what most people come into contact with a formal instruction and explanation of science for the first time, at least in a systematic way. (3) It is at this point which the foundations are laid for an interest in science. What is taught (and how) in this first encounter will largely determine an individual's view of the subject in adult life.

(4) Understanding the original of the negative attitudes towards science may help us to modify them. (5) Most education system neglect exploration, understanding and reflection. (6) Teachers in schools tend to present science as a collection of facts, often by more detail than necessary. (7) As a result, children memorize processes such as mathematical formulas or the periodic table, only to forget it shortly afterwards. (8) The task of learning facts and concepts, one at a time, makes learning laborious, boring and efficient. Such a purely empirical approach, which consists of observation and description, is also, in a sense, unscientific or incomplete. (9) There is therefore a need for resources and methods of teaching that facilitates a deep understanding of science in an enjoyable way. (10) Science should not only be "fun" in the same way as playing a video game, but "hard fun"—deep feeling of connection made possibly only by imaginative engagement.

(1) _____　(2) _____　(3) _____　(4) _____　(5) _____

(6) _____　(7) _____　(8) _____　(9) _____　(10) _____

Part IV　Writing

Directions: Develop each of the following topics into an essay of about 200 words.

1. Effects of Science and Technology on Human Life

2. High-tech, a Blessing or a Curse?

3. Technology—a Double-edged Sword

Section B Extensive Reading and Translation

Basic Research and Graduate Education

By Glenn Seaborg

[1] Basic research is the cutting of paths through the unknown. As most of us know today, it is the pacesetter for technology and the raw material invention.

[2] (1) <u>Because basic research is aimed at understanding rather than at practical results, the layman sometimes assumes that it is entirely abstract and theoretical, and that only when it becomes a matter of industrial development does it "come down to earth".</u>

This is a false notion, and its falsity becomes increasingly clear with time. Indeed, one striking characteristic of our scientific age has been the disappearance of the barriers between pure and applied science. (2) <u>Not only are we finding important technological application for mathematical and scientific knowledge which was formerly thought of as abstract and "useless", but the advance of technology has both generated new problems in pure science and provided new tools with which such science can be advanced more effectively.</u> The development of the techniques and hardware for radar during the war, for example, gave the physicist and the chemist a new and refined tool for investigating the properties of solids and of chemical compounds. Conversely, the extensive use of this tool in basic science has opened the way to entirely new techniques in electronics. Similarly, the development of large-scale electronic computers has led engineers to find practical uses for some of the most abstruse and "impractical" branches of higher mathematics, while the understanding of the techniques of using computers has, on the other hand, given us deeper insight into some aspects of the behavior of complex biological and social systems. Basic and applied science today are distinguished less by method and content than by motivation. Very often, indeed, the same man can be both "pure scientist" and "engineer", as he works on different problems or on different parts of one problem.

[3] By the word scientist we mean someone who is fit to take part in basic research, to learn without a teacher, to discover and attack significant problems not yet solved, to show the nature of this process to others—someone, in short, who is equipped to spend a lifetime in the advancement of science, to the best of his ability.

[4] The process of graduate education and the process of basic research belong together at every possible level. The two kinds of activity reinforce each other in a great variety of ways, and each is

weakened when carried on without the other.

[5] (3) If graduate education aims at making scientists, and if inquiry into what is unknown is the moving principle of all science, it is not surprising that experience of this kind of inquiry should be essential in graduate education. Clearly such experience is best obtained in association with others who have had it or are having it themselves. The apprentice scientist learns best when he learns in an atmosphere of active research work. In all forms of scientific work a man's effectiveness is multiplied when he has that depth of understanding of his subject that comes only with the experience of working at a research problem.

[6] The process of graduate education depends on "research" just as much as upon "teaching"—indeed, the two are essentially inseparable—and there is a radical error in trying to think of them as different or opposite forms of activity. From the point of view of the graduate student, the teaching and the research of his professor are, at the crucial point which defines the whole, united. What he learns is not opposite from research; it is research. (4) Of course many necessary parts of a scientist's education have little to do with research, and obviously, also, for many professors there must be a gap between teaching a standard graduate course and working at one's own problems. Moreover, many good teachers—men who keep up with the new work in their subject and communicate its meaning clearly to their students—are not themselves engaged in research. Yet we insist on the central point: the would-be scientist must learn what it is like to do science, and this, which is research, is the most important thing he can be "taught".

[7] So far we have been arguing that graduate education requires the experience of basic research. What happens when we turn the matter around, and ask whether basic research must be carried on only in conjunction with graduate education? Here the answer cannot be so categorical. (5) Though our general conviction is that a fundamentally reciprocal relation does exist, it is clear that research of outstanding quality is often carried on in isolation from teaching and indeed quite outside the universities. While the great teacher of graduate students is almost invariably a research man too, there are many notable scientists who have as little as possible to do with teaching. First-rate industrial and governmental laboratories with commitments to specific programs are necessarily separated in some measure from teaching of a conventional sort. Thus, basic research can be, and is, carried on without much connection to graduate education.

[8] Yet in the long run it is dangerous to separate research in any field entirely from education. The pool of graduate students in our universities is the pool from which the scientist of the future must come. These young people do not easily study what is not taught; they do not often learn the meaning of research which does not exist in their environment. A scientific field which has no research life in the universities is at a grave disadvantage in recruiting new members. As learning and teaching require research, so research, in the end, cannot be sustained without teaching. Hence it is always important for research installations to maintain effective connections with students.

[9] There is also the fact that in the wider sense all first-rate research laboratories are permeated by an atmosphere of learning. Successful research can be defined, indeed, as learning what has not been taught before, and a good scientist is constantly learning from others. We believe that research, learning and teaching are deeply connected processes which should be kept together wherever possible.

Part A　Translate English into Chinese

I. Translate the underlined sentences in the above text into Chinese.

II. Translate paragraphs 8, 9 in the above text into Chinese.

Part B　Translate Chinese into English

I. Translate the following sentences into English with the words or phrases in the passage in Section B.

1. 金属的某些性质对工程师来说很重要,各种各样的方法被用来研究这些性质。

2. 工作态度不端正,或者缺乏必要的人际交往能力,一个人就不会尽其所能去做事。

3. 面对未来的市场竞争,实施绿色营销是企业增强自身竞争力的最佳选择。

4. 系统地观察动物的异常行为,结合其他方法,可用来预测大规模的具有毁坏性的地震。

5. 在当下人们普遍认为科学与技术密不可分,且认为两者自古以来就是如此。

II. Translate the following paragraph into English.

　　作者认为,理论科学主要涉及那些一般称为模式的学说的发展。这些学说是用来证实宇宙现象之间的关系。另一方面,应用科学则直接关系到如何把理论科学的通用定律应用到生活的实际事物中去,应用到加强人类对环境的控制上去,从而使新技术、新方法和新机械得到发展。十分明显,应用科学是纯理论工作和实验工作的实际延伸。这说明,理论科学和应用科学是相互依赖、相互影响的。

Unit 9

Section A   Intensive Reading and Writing

Feeling Guilty

Arthur Dobrin

[1] Many thoughtful parents want to shield their children from feelings of guilt or shame in much the same way that they want to spare them from fear. Guilt and shame as methods of discipline are to be eschewed along with raised hands and leather straps. Fear, guilt and shame as methods of moral instruction are seen as failures in decent parenting. Parents want their children to be happy and how can you feel happy when you are feeling guilty, fearful or ashamed? If we were really convinced that using fear, guilt or shame as methods of discipline worked, though, we might be more ready to use them as techniques. But we aren't convinced that this is the case. We won't have more socially responsible people if fear, guilt and shame are part of their disciplinary diet as children.

[2] Instead, we will simply have unhappy people. Responsible behavior has nothing to do with the traditional methods of raising moral children. This doesn't mean that guilt isn't an important feeling. It is. Guilt helps keep people on the right moral track. But guilt is a derivative emotion, one that follows from having violated an internalized moral standard. This is far different than making someone feel guilty in order to create the standard in the first instance.

[3] My wife once edited a magazine about hunger. A view held by many associated with the sponsoring organization claimed, You can't get people to give money to starving children by making them feel guilty. So the magazine didn't show pictures of starving children, children with doleful eyes. Instead, there were photos of women in the fields, portraits of peasant farmers and pictures of

political organizers. But the publishers weren't completely right about believing that guilt-inducing pictures don't lead to moral action. In fact, it was the graphic pictures of starving children in Somalia that called the world's attention to the dire situation there. The power of television is that it does bring images of others' tragedies directly into our home. No rational analysis can do the same. When we are moved to pity, we should also be moved to action.

[4] If we don't do anything, then we feel guilty. We become part of the problem we see and feel guilty for letting bad things happen to people. How can I, good person that I am, let this continue? What has pricked the conscience here are guilty feelings.

[5] Perhaps the most famous account of the origins of guilt is Freud's[1] *Civilization and Its Discontents*. His theory is that guilt arises because there is a conflict between the demands of civilization and that of an individual's instincts. In Freud's view, inside each person there is a seething cauldron bubbling with sexual passion. No society can survive if people acted upon this instinct at will, so we have laws which put a lid on libidinous behavior. But that doesn't make the sexual drive go away. It merely represses it. This creates a serious problem, though, since humans also have a need to release their tensions. What we have, then, is an ongoing conflict between passion and the law, between sexual energy and society. Civilization, Freud says, exists upon the very discontent it has created.

[6] The analysis doesn't rest there. Freud goes farther by noting that most of us, as adults, don't experience civilization as something external to ourselves. Rather we take it in as an active part of our very being. We internalize the voices that told us as children, Don't do that; no, you can't have that. This internalized voice is the superego. It functions as society's watchdog and it watches over us, Freud writes, like a garrison in a conquered city. The importance of the superego, from society's perspective, is that it acts in place of parents, courts and the police. When it is operating fully, a person doesn't even need society to punish him for his misdeeds. Our guilty consciences make us feel terrible enough, so bad that we won't make the same mistake again.

[7] The process operates largely unnoticed, as it exists in part in our unconscious minds. Our sense of guilt, then, is a result of suppressing our instinctive natures for the sake of the larger good we call civilization. Freud thought this was inevitable and even necessary. Guilt is the price for having a conscience.

[8] Guilty feelings arise when we have violated a moral norm that we accept as valid. A person who feels guilty, notes philosopher Herbert Morris[2], is one who has internalized norms and, as such, is committed to avoiding wrong. The mere fact that the wrong is believed to have occurred, regardless of who bears responsibility for it, naturally causes distress. When we are attached to a person, injury to that person causes us pain regardless of who or what has occasioned the injury. We needn't believe that we had control over hurting (or not helping) another person in order to feel guilty.

[9] Psychologists Nico Frijda and Batja Mesquita[3] of the University of Amsterdam find that people feel guilty about having harmed someone even when it was accidental. Nearly half the people they interviewed felt guilty for having caused unintended harm, such as hurting one's mother when leaving home to marry.

[10] Unintentional harm may lead to as strong guilt feelings as intentional harm. In other

words, being careless is as much a source of guilt as intentional harm. We say, If only I had been more careful, If only I had paid more attention, If only I were a better driver. The fact that a court may not even bring charges against you in the first place may help to assuage some of the pain but it doesn't remove all the feelings of guilt.

[11] The feeling is useful in so far as it makes us more cautious, makes us better drivers or moves us to socially responsible action. The sociopath never experiences such feelings and therefore poses a danger to society; the neurotic experiences so much of it that he can't function normally in society.

[12] Feeling guilty for harm you have caused when you aren't responsible is possible because there is a more generalized readiness to accept responsibility for your actions. Guilt arises when we think we have had choices and then have made the wrong moral choice. Guilt and responsibility appear to go together. If we do harm and feel no guilt, then we don't believe we are responsible for what we've done. This means that we see ourselves as victims—of circumstances, of coercion, of ignorance and so forth.

[13] Remember that people who think of themselves as victims do so because they believe they have no control over events in their lives. They don't feel responsible and therefore don't feel guilty either. Several tactics can be used in disavowing responsibility: following the crowd, it is someone else's problem, it was done under duress.

[14] Some eschew responsibility by claiming that they had nothing to do with the situation. It's not my problem, is the refrain. I have heard people decry the state of the environment as they get into their cars to drive a few blocks to the supermarket for a small bag of groceries or people who complain about rudeness on the part of youngsters and have no compunctions about mistreating waiters. They refuse to see their part and by refusing to see, feel no responsibility. These people then claim the moral high ground without having a rightful claim to it. They feel good in their self-righteousness.

[15] None of us is perfect and that we live in an imperfect world. This means that we can't avoid hurting others. As the Japanese poet Shuntaro Tanikawa[4] expresses it:

As surely as the earth turns, we will do harm again. In the silence of our hearts...there we must make a promise to ourselves, a promise we must try to keep. This is the promise to harm less often, speak less sharply, tear less cruelly. Only we can repair the tears, mend that which we have rent.

[16] If we accept this, then we have to accept guilt feelings as a consequence of being moral people.

[17] Guilt has its place in morality. The Oliners (researchers who studied what made some Germans rescue Jews during the Holocaust[5] despite great personal risk), found that about half the rescuers of Jews were motivated by guilt. But guilt that leads to responsible behavior results from violating moral standards that have been accepted and internalized by a person. The work of Leo Montada[6] bears directly on this point. He studied what he terms existential guilt.

[18] This kind of guilt arises when, for example, a person is the sole survivor of an accident or escapes persecution or survives a concentration camp. Primo Levi[7] was so consumed by this pervading sense of guilt, having lived through the Holocaust as an Italian Jew, that he committed suicide

decades later. This feeling is easy to understand when the survivor was close to those who perished.

[19] Leo Montada wanted to know if such guilt is also felt in less extreme circumstances and whether it is experienced in regard to socially distant individuals or strangers. He found that three factors were necessary to produce such guilt: they accepted the fact that there were people less fortunate than themselves; they believed that the needy were not deserving of their fate; and they believed that their well-being was linked to another's misfortune. And the guilt they experienced motivated them to take action on behalf of the needy. In other words, those who felt guilt already had a set of ethical values.

[20] The clear conclusion from the studies on guilt is that attempting to induce guilt as a means of creating a moral standard that will be accepted by the individual is bound to fail. The process is backwards. Guilt flows from morality, not the other way around. If people feel guilty when they have done wrong, it is because they already possess a moral compass. But if they are lacking the rudiments of moral feelings and don't possess mature moral judgment, then deliberately instilling guilt won't create an ethical person. Instead it will more likely create an angry, hostile person.

Notes to the Text

1. **Sigmund Freud** (1856—1939)—Austrian physician and neurologist, founder of psychoanalysis, a new school of psychology embodying revolutionary and controversial views of human behavior. He also established a new system for treating behavior disorders. Freudian theory had a great effect on psychology, psychiatry and other fields. His works include *The Interpretation of Dreams* (1899), *Three Essays on the Theory of Sexuality* (1905), and *Civilization and its Discontents* (1930). The last one revealed the essential weaknesses in human society and indicated much that needs to be remedied.

2. **Herbert Morris** (1928—)—Philosopher. His works are *Freedom and Responsibility: Readings in Philosophy and Law* (1961), *Guilt and Shame* (1971), and *The Masked Citadel: The Significance of the Title of Stendhal's La Chartreuse de Parme* (1968).

3. **Nico Frijda & Batja Mesquita**—Psychologists of the University of Amsterdam. Some of Nico Frijda's works are as follows: *Appraisal and Beyond: The Issue of Cognitive Determinates of Emotion* (1993, co-ed.), *Emotions and Beliefs: How Feelings Influence Thoughts* (2000, co-ed).

4. **Shuntarō Tanikawa**—(谷川俊太郎)(born December 15, 1931 in Tokyo City, Japan)—a Japanese poet and translator. He is one of the most widely read and highly regarded of living Japanese poets, both in Japan and abroad, and a frequent subject of speculations regarding the Nobel Prize in Literature. Several of his collections, including his selected works, have been translated into English, and his *Floating the River in Melancholy*, translated by William I. Eliot and Kazuo Kawamura, won the American Book Award in 1989.

5. **the Holocaust**—It's a term for the methodical persecution, enslavement and extermination of European Jewry by Nazi Germany. As estimated 6 million Jews died in the years from 1933 to 1945. Europe had a history of anti-Semitism, but the Holocaust was unique in scope, barbarity,

and concentration on the annihilation of one people. Moreover, anti-Semitism was given legal sanction. The Holocaust was directed by the Nazi director Adolf Hitler.

6. **Leo Montada**—His works include *Life Crises and Experiences of Loss in Adulthood* (1992, co-ed), *Current Societal Concerns about Justice* (1996, co-ed), and *Responses to Victimization and Belief in a Just World* (1998, co-ed).

7. **Primo Levi** (July 31, 1919-April 11, 1987)—A survivor of the Holocaust, an Italian Jewish chemist and writer. He was the author of two novels and several collections of short stories, essays, and poems, but is best known for *If This Is a Man*, his account of the year he spent as a prisoner in the Auschwitz concentration camp in Nazi-occupied Poland. His works include *Other People's Trade* (1989), *The Mirror Maker: Stories and Essays* (1989), and *Survival in Auschwitz: The Nazi Assault on Humanity* (1996).

Part I   Comprehension of the Text

1. What does the title possibly mean?
2. In what situations are people likely to feel guilty?
3. What does the writer mean by "Guilt is the price for having a conscience"?
4. The legal system often protects the names of those found guilty. To name the guilty is to shame them. What's your opinion towards publicly naming the guilty?
5. What is the author's conclusion?

Part II   Vocabulary

A. Choose the one from the four choices that best explains the underlined word or phrase.

1. The competition for top employees is heating up even as companies eschew old training methods.
   A. induce   B. avoid   C. enchant   D. shield

2. If you make a contract under duress or undue influence, you lack the free will to choose and consent.
   A. coercion   B. conviction   C. concession   D. oppression

3. The legacy of those who have perished is present every day in our work and inspires generations of new space explorers.
   A. injured   B. vanished   C. survived   D. died

4. Pressure is mounting on the monetary policy committee to lift rates from 0.5 per cent to put a lid on the soaring prices.
   A. regulate   B. restrict   C. resist   D. refrain

5. The sight of their suffering may have pricked his conscience because he was living in Egyptian comfort and luxury.
   A. scared   B. obscured   C. pierced   D. screwed

6. Every composer knows the anguish and despair <u>occasioned</u> by forgetting ideas which one had no time to write down.

A. initiated   B. caused   C. extended   D. depicted

7. When a company is experiencing financial <u>distress</u>, the book values and the market values of liabilities carried by the firm can differ.

A. discontent   B. jealousy   C. sorrow   D. hatred

8. The United States publicly <u>disavowed</u> South Korean incorporation into the Asian defensive sphere.

A. denied   B. deserted   C. divorced   D. seethed

9. Chief executives start making pleasant speeches and smile a lot because they want to <u>assuage</u> the concerns of their borrowers.

A. alleviate   B. eliminate   C. diminish   D. transform

10. In the mid-nineteenth century, opium-smoking was <u>decried</u> as a major social and public health problem, especially in the West.

A. overrated   B. complained   C. reprimanded   D. condemned

B. Choose the one from the four choices that best completes the sentence.

1. Finding it hard to _____ a smile, Rose reverted her attention to the paper crane in her lap.

A. repress   B. suppress   C. depress   D. impress

2. She hasn't the slightest _____ in admitting that she has occasionally violated her own standards.

A. compunction   B. complaint   C. compassion   D. compulsion

3. In the journey of life, if you want to travel without fear, you must have the ticket of a good _____.

A. coherence   B. consensus   C. conscience   D. conscious

4. The reason corruption has _____ in all systems of our society is that we as citizens are not aware of our political rights.

A. penetrated   B. perished   C. perceived   D. pervaded

5. He wants to _____ a pride in their work in a place where everyone is treated with respect and their suggestions are appreciated.

A. install   B. distill   C. instill   D. entail

6. They don't know what to do and don't even know how to listen to their own heart since they used to just blindly _____ the crowd.

A. follow   B. observe   C. pursue   D. flow

7. We are _____ to protecting and respecting your privacy and to using technology to enhance your online security.

A. entitled   B. bound   C. committed   D. honored

8. Some people welcome them for their intensity and excitement; some people fear them as they _____ guilt and shame.

A. deduce   B. induce   C. seduce   D. reduce

9. Mostly youngsters are preferred in this field as they have new ideas, concepts and are _____ with enthusiasm.

A. grumbling   B. stumbling   C. bubbling   D. mumbling

10. The primary _____ factors affecting industries include technology, government, social changes, demographics and foreign influences.

    A. interior   B. exterior   C. internal   D. external

C. Complete each sentence with the proper form of the word given in the parenthesis.

1. Anger is usually a _____ feeling from another, and in the instance of a major change, it can appear seemingly out of nowhere. (derive)

2. Americans have _____ the value that mothers of young children should be mothers first and foremost, and not paid workers. (internal)

3. Animals of all classes, old and young, shrink with _____ fear from any strange object approaching them. (instinct)

4. The most _____ experience you can have is to work for someone who trusts you and who gives you the freedom to grow. (fortune)

5. The wider public sentiment appears to be one of growing _____ with the growth of local governments chasing revenue through land sales. (content)

6. Little is known about the impact that non-parental care has on childhood _____ injury and whether this varies by socio-economic group. (intend)

7. Its only value is as a case study on how _____ customers will kill even the most dominant brand. (treat)

8. The current work explored the conditions under which infants _____ spatial relationships from one event to another. (general)

9. Caution should be used whenever _____ action is being considered for an employee's use of sick leave. (discipline)

10. The character is revealed, not by occasional good deeds and occasional _____, but by the tendency of the habitual words and acts. (deed)

Part III   Cloze

Directions: There are totally 20 blanks in the following passage. Fill in each blank with one word only.

Two elderly women in my community died "full of years", which means both died __1__ the normal wearing out of the body after a long and full life. Their homes happened to be near each other, so I __2__ visits to the families.

The son of one of the deceased women said to me, "If __3__ I had sent my mother to Florida and got her out of this cold, she would be alive today". The son of the __4__ deceased woman said, "If only I hadn't insisted __5__ my mother's going to Florida, she would be __6__ today. That long airplane ride, the sudden __7__ of climate, was more than she could take".

When things don't turn out __8__ we would like them to, it is very likely for us to think that if we had done things __9__, the story would have had a happier ending. Any time there is a death, the

  10   will feel guilty.

There seem to be two   11   in our readiness to feel guilty. The first is our pressing need to believe that the world   12   sense and that there is a cause for every effect and a reason   13   everything that happens. That leads us to try to find the patterns and connections.

The second element is the   14   that we are the cause of what happens,   15   the bad things that happen. Psychologists   16   this feeling back to our childhood. A baby   17   to think that the world exists to meet his needs, and   18   he makes everything happen in it. The world works for him. When he cries, someone comes to   19   to him. When he is   20 , the people feed him, and when he is wet, people change him. Very often, we do not completely outgrow the notion that our wishes cause things to happen.

Part IV   Writing

Directions: Develop each of the following topics into an essay of about 200 words.
1. Is Cheating on Exam Guilty?
2. On Happiness
3. A guilty conscience needs no accuser. Interpret your understanding of the proverb.

Section B Extensive Reading and Translation

What Makes People Unhappy?

By Bertrand Russell

[1] Animals are happy so long as they have health and enough to eat. Human beings, one feels, ought to be, but in the modern world they are not, at least in a great majority of cases. If you are unhappy yourself, you will probably be prepared to admit that you are not exceptional in this. If you are happy, ask yourself how many of your friends are so. And when you have reviewed your friends, teach yourself the art of reading faces; make yourself receptive to the moods of those whom you meet in the course of an ordinary day.

[2] Though the kinds are different, you will find that unhappiness meets you everywhere. Let us suppose that you are in New York, the most typically modern of the great cities. (1) Stand in a busy street during working hours, or on a main thoroughfare on the weekend, or at a dance in the evening; empty your mind of your own ego, and let the personalities of the strangers about you take possession of you, one after another. You will find that each of these different crowds has its own troubles. In the work-hour crowd you will see anxiety, excessive concentration, dyspepsia, lack of interest in anything but the struggle, incapacity for play, unconsciousness of their fellow creatures. On a main road at the weekend you will see men and women, all comfortably off, and some very rich, engaged in the pursuit of pleasure.

[3] Or, again, watch people at a gay evening. All come determined to be happy, with the kind of grim resolve with which one determines not to make a fuss at the dentist's. (2) It is held that drink and petting are the gateways to joy, so people get drunk quickly, and try not to notice how much their partners disgust them. After a sufficient amount of drink, men begin to weep, and to lament how unworthy they are, morally, of the devotion of their mothers. All that alcohol does for them is to liberate the sense of sin, which reason suppresses in saner moments.

[4] The causes of these various kinds of unhappiness lie partly in the social system, partly in individual psychology—which, of course, is itself to a considerable extent a product of the social system. To discover a system for the avoidance of war is a vital need for our civilization; but no such system has a chance while men are so unhappy that mutual extermination seems to them less dreadful than continued endurance of the light of day. What can a man or woman, here and now, in the midst of our nostalgic society, do to achieve happiness for himself or herself?

[5] My purpose is to suggest a cure for the ordinary day-to-day unhappiness from which most

people in civilized countries suffer, and which is all the more unbearable because, having no obvious external cause, it appears inescapable. (4) I believe this unhappiness to be very largely due to mistaken views of the world, mistaken ethics, mistaken habits of life, leading to destruction of that natural zest and appetite for possible things upon which all happiness, whether of men or animals, ultimately depends. These are matters which lie within the power of the individual, and I propose to suggest the changes by which his happiness, given average good fortune, may be achieved.

[6] Perhaps the best introduction to the philosophy which I wish to advocate will be a few words of autobiography. I was not born happy. As a child, my favorite hymn was: 'Weary of earth and laden with my sin'. At the age of five, I reflected that, if I should live to be seventy, I had only endured, so far, a fourteenth part of my whole life, and I felt the long-spread-out boredom ahead of me to be almost unendurable. In adolescence, I hated life and was continually on the verge of suicide, from which, however, I was restrained by the desire to know more mathematics.

[7] Now, on the contrary, I enjoy life; I might almost say that with every year that passes I enjoy it more. This is due partly to having discovered what the things that I most desired were and having gradually acquired many of these things. Partly it is due to having successfully dismissed certain objects of desire—such as the acquisition of indubitable knowledge about something or other—as essentially unattainable. But very largely it is due to a diminishing preoccupation with myself.

[8] Gradually I learned to be indifferent to myself and my deficiencies; I came to centre my attention increasingly upon external objects: the state of the world, various branches of knowledge, individuals for whom I felt affection. External interests, it is true, bring each its own possibility of pain: the world may be plunged in war, knowledge in some direction may be hard to achieve, friends may die. But pains of these kinds do not destroy the essential quality of life, as do those that spring from disgust with self. And every external interest inspires some activity which, so long as the interest remains alive, is a complete preventive of ennui. Interest in oneself, on the contrary, leads to no activity of a progressive kind. It may lead to the keeping of a diary, to getting psycho-analyzed, or perhaps to becoming a monk. But the monk will not be happy until the routine of the monastery has made him forget his own soul. The happiness which he attributes to religion he could have obtained from becoming a crossing-sweeper, provided he were compelled to remain one. External discipline is the only road to happiness for those unfortunates whose self-absorption is too profound to be cured in any other way.

[9] The psychological causes of unhappiness, it is clear, are many and various. But all have something in common. (4) The typical unhappy man is one who, having been deprived in youth of some normal satisfaction, has come to value this one kind of satisfaction more than any other, and has therefore given to his life a one-sided direction, together with a quite undue emphasis upon the achievement as opposed to the activities connected with it. There is, however, a further development which is very common in the present day. A man may feel so completely thwarted that he seeks no form of satisfaction, but only distraction and oblivion. He then becomes a devotee of 'pleasure'. That is to say he seeks to make life bearable by becoming less alive. Drunkenness, for example, is temporary suicide; the happiness that it brings is merely negative, a momentary cessation of unhappiness. The narcissist and the megalomaniac believe that happiness is possible, though they

may adopt mistaken means of achieving it; but the man who seeks intoxication, in whatever form, has given up hope except in oblivion. In his case, the first thing to be done is to persuade him that happiness is desirable. (5) Men, who are unhappy, like men who sleep badly, are always proud of the fact. Perhaps their pride is like that of the fox who had lost his tail; if so, the way to cure it is to point out to them how they can grow a new tail. Very few men, I believe, will deliberately choose unhappiness if they see a way of being happy. I do not deny that such men exist, but they are not sufficiently numerous to be important. I shall therefore assume that the reader would rather be happy than unhappy. Whether I can help him to realize this wish, I do not know; but at any rate the attempt can do no harm.

Part A Translate English into Chinese

I. Translate the underlined sentences in the above text into Chinese.

II. Translate paragraph 8 in the above text into Chinese.

Part B Translate Chinese into English

I. Translate the following sentences into English with the words or phrases in the passage in Section B.

1. 精彩纷呈的文化活动,智慧迭出的论坛研讨,让我们认识到人类对美好生活的理解与追求引领城市发展。

2. 若非你及时伸出援助之手,本公司将会濒临破产的边缘。

3. 科学家和研究人员都强烈反对这一理论,并认为他的主张荒谬可笑而不予以考虑。

4. 比起在宿舍里学习来,我在图书馆里收益要大得多,宿舍里的干扰太大了。

5. 对未来的关注不仅使我们看不到现在是什么样子,而且还常使我们重新整理过去。

II. Translate the following paragraphs into English.

　　你曾为做了不该做或应该做却没有做的事而后悔过吗? 或许我们曾经都有过这种经历。当然现在为此沮丧已经没有任何意义了——后悔无用。然而,我们在正确思考所发生的事情及其原因时或许会有所收获,因为我们也许能从中得出一些会对以后有用的结论。

　　我们不时都会做的一件事就是:向我们的朋友或亲人发脾气。奇怪的是我们向喜欢的人发脾气比向陌生人发脾气的时候要多一些。理由或许就是我们把朋友或亲人看成一个安全的保证,一个可以在安全的环境下发泄一下的机会,而冒犯陌生人的后果则可能会严重得多。

Unit 10

Section A　Intensive Reading and Writing

Flag Fever: the Paradox of Patriotism

By Blaine Harden

[1] UNTIL it was uncorked by acts of war on Sept. 11, generations of Americans had never found a compelling reason to take a stiff drink of patriotism or take comfort in its unifying high.

[2] With an ennobling wallop, patriotism has since inspired a deeply felt and classless sense of community. Charitable gifts have skyrocketed, as have sales of flags and stocks of donated blood. Firemen and police officers, who define themselves by sacrifice and service rather than by status and stock options, have become objects of mass adulation. According to some reports, irony has died.

[3] New York City, the erstwhile epicenter of selfishness and sin, has been judged in its time of trial and found good by more than 8 out of 10 Americans. Perhaps boundaries were melting between the Red Zone, the conservative heartland that voted for the Republican president, and the Blue Zone, where coastal liberals had clung to doubts about President Bush's work ethic, his judgment and his intelligence.

[4] Yet, from the moment suicide terrorists steered airplanes into the World Trade Center[1] and the Pentagon[2], the invidious paradox of American patriotism came back into play. Constitutional rights, which supposedly form the core of patriotism's appeal, suddenly lost ground to fear. As it has during every major military conflict since World War I, a nationalist undertow that is culturally conformist, ethnically exclusive and belligerently militaristic began to silence dissent, spread fear among immigrants and lock up people without explanation.

[5] The White House press secretary, Ari Fleischer, warned reporters that in times like these "people have to watch what they say and watch what they do". In lock step with times like these,

loose lips have been slapped shut. As an Oregon columnist, a University of New Mexico professor and a late-night talk show host all discovered last week, the country is suddenly thick with self-appointed censors. They are firing, disciplining and pulling advertising from those whose commentary or jokes sound insufficiently loyal.

[6] Patriotism's extraordinary power to expand and constrain the American spirit is hardly new. But it seems novel now because so many people—including many among that huge bulge of the population that came of age during and after the Vietnam War—have never lived it themselves.

[7] A heartfelt and reinvigorating love of country has not been universally experienced in the United States since the Kennedy assassination[3], said Gary Gerstle, a professor of history at the University of Maryland and author of "American Crucible: Race and Nation in the Twentieth Century" (Princeton University Press, 2001). "After the civil rights movement[4] and the war in Vietnam, there was a sustained cultural crisis", he said. "Many Americans did not waver, but a lot did. They asked, 'Who are we?' 'Are we good?' What is emerging now is something completely different. It's a broadly based consensus on the value of America."

[8] Patriotism seems particularly potent and purely felt among the tens of millions of Americans who came of age after the 1960's and early 70's. Unlike many of their parents, they can wave the flag without the mixed feelings of a generation that did its darndest to dodge military service in an unpopular war and, in more than a few cases, burned flags rather than waved them. Unburdened by such memories—the wars of the 90's were all too short and decisive to stir such passions—Americans under 40 suddenly have a chance to reimagine themselves, to participate selflessly in a world-rousing conflict that might define them as something other than Generation X, Y or Z.

[9] For all its ennobling kick, historians agree that patriotism has almost always been at odds with itself. It reinforces a sense of community by erecting strong walls to comfort those on the inside. But outside those exclusive walls, it has a history of denying equal protection under the law and making life seem scary.

[10] The flag, as much as any symbol, embodies the paradox. As surprisingly reassuring as it has been to many baby boomers who had never before viewed themselves as flag-wavers, it has been unnerving for Arab-Americans and other immigrant groups, like Sikhs. "I see flags everywhere, yet my first instinct is apprehension", said Nabeel Abraham, an American-born anthropologist of Palestinian descent who is a co-author of "Arab Detroit" (Wayne State University Press, 2000), an examination of the country's oldest and largest Arab-American community. He said most Arab-Americans and many Asians who could be mistaken for Arabs are staying home as much as possible and keeping quiet. "We don't know what to expect", he said. "We expect the worst."

[11] For other Americans, not just those whose ethnicity make them feel coerced by patriotism, the proliferation of flags and "God Bless America" signage can seem a bit too simplistic, a feel-good distraction from trying to understand a monstrously precise act of simultaneous suicide.

[12] A contentious and still unresolved struggle over what the flag should symbolize has been going on since at least 1863, when President Lincoln issued the Emancipation Proclamation[5]. Since then, according to Cecilia Elizabeth O'Leary, a history professor at California State University in Monterey Bay, there have been Americans who define the flag as primarily a symbol of equal rights

and social justice under the law. It was not until World War I, she said, when federal and state governments joined forces with right-wing organizations and vigilantes, that the flag's egalitarian resonance was drowned out by jingoism.

[13] In 1918, a Montana court sentenced E. V. Starr to 20 years in prison for refusing to kiss a flag. As Professor O'Leary noted in "To Die For: The Paradox of American Patriotism" (Princeton University Press, 1999), an appeals judge reluctantly decided he could not reverse the sentence. But he did condemn the way that patriotism, with the approval of government authorities, had devolved into a kind of "fanaticism".

[14] Since then, the strength of exclusionary patriotism has waxed and waned, usually as a corollary of fear, with abuses most widespread when the federal government plays a supporting role. In the frenzy that followed World War I, the Palmer raids[6], led by an attorney general whose house had been bombed, included the detention, beatings and deportations of thousands of people, most of them immigrants. Each successive war featured its own shameful excess. World War II had the internment of 110,000 Japanese, the Korean War coincided with McCarthyism[7], and during the Vietnam conflict the F. B. I. infiltrated antiwar groups.

[15] Less than three weeks into America's latest flush of flag-waving fervor, it's too early to know if patriotism's undertow will cause systemic abuses of civil liberties. The signals, so far, are mixed.

[16] The Bush administration's request for authority to detain suspected terrorists indefinitely has run into opposition from senior Democrats and Republicans in Congress. Even harsh critics of the administration, like Michael Maggio, an immigration expert, say the White House seems to be able to sense when it has gone too far.

[17] "I have been impressed by the administration's willingness to back away from some of its most outlandish proposals", he said, referring to an earlier plan, now discarded, to deport foreign-born legal residents suspected of terrorist involvement.

[18] Perhaps most reassuring, for Americans who thirst for a brand of patriotism that elevates their spirits and protects minorities, are President Bush's repeated calls for ethnic and religious tolerance, along with his highly publicized meetings with Arab, Muslim and Sikh leaders.

[19] "As long as this continues, it bodes well for inclusion and tolerance", said Professor Gerstle, at the University of Maryland. "But this is a very fluid moment. What happens if another airliner hits a building? Many people are going to be out for revenge if American boys get killed. "

[20] The worst abuses against immigrant Americans occurred not at the beginning of World War I, but at the end, when the federal government lost touch with Constitutional protections and briefly joined forces with the mob.

[21] President Bush and his senior advisers have warned Americans to expect a war that is long, murky and unsatisfying. As months stretch into years, it is also likely to be a conflict that periodically screams for the clarifying blood of a scapegoat. If the president is going to continue to insist on an inclusive kind of patriotism, home-front defense of tolerance could prove as formidable as the war itself.

Notes to the Text

1. **World Trade Center** (**WTC**)—a complex of seven buildings in Lower Manhattan in New York City that was destroyed in the September 11, 2001 terrorist attacks. The site is currently being rebuilt with six new skyscrapers and a memorial to the casualties of the attacks. The original World Trade Center was designed by Minoru Yamasaki in the early 1960s using a tube-frame structural design for the twin 110-story towers. Groundbreaking for the World Trade Center took place on August 5, 1966. The North Tower (1) was completed in December 1972 and the South Tower (2) was finished in July 1973; the two were collectively known as the **Twin Towers**, the two tallest buildings in Manhattan at that time. On the morning of September 11, 2001, Al-Qaeda-affiliated hijackers flew two 767 jets into the complex, one into each tower, in a coordinated terrorist attack. After burning for 56 minutes, the South Tower (2) collapsed, followed a half-hour later by the North Tower (1), with the attacks on the World Trade Center resulting in 2,752 deaths.

2. **The Pentagon**—the headquarters of the United States Department of Defense, located in Arlington County, Virginia. As a symbol of the U.S. military, "the Pentagon" is often used metonymically to refer to the Department of Defense rather than the building itself. Designed by the American architect George Bergstrom (1876—1955), and built by Philadelphia, Pennsylvania, general contractor John McShain, the building was dedicated on January 15, 1943, after ground was broken for construction on September 11, 1941. On September 11, 2001, exactly 60 years after the building's groundbreaking, hijacked American Airlines Flight 77 was crashed into the western side of the Pentagon, killing 189 people, including five hijackers, 59 others aboard the plane, and 125 working in the building

3. **The Kennedy assassination—John Fitzgerald Kennedy**, the thirty-fifth President of the United States, was assassinated at 12:30 p.m. Central Standard Time (18:30 UTC) on Friday, November 22, 1963, in Dealey Plaza, Dallas, Texas. Kennedy was fatally shot while traveling with his wife Jacqueline, Texas governor John Connally, and the latter's wife, Nellie, in a Presidential motorcade.

4. **The civil rights movement**—The basis for civil rights in the US is the Constitution and its first 10 amendments, the BILL OF RIGHT. This deals, for example, with freedom of speech, press, religion and assembly, freedom from unreasonable seizure and searches, right to a speedy public trial; and prohibition of double jeopardy and self-incrimination.

5. **Emancipation Proclamation**—an executive order issued by United States President Abraham Lincoln on January 1, 1863, during the American Civil War under his war powers. It proclaimed the freedom of 3.1 million of the nation's 4 million slaves, and immediately freed 50,000 of them, with the rest freed as Union armies advanced. The Proclamation made abolition a central goal of the war (in addition to reunion), angered many Northern Democrats, energized anti-slavery forces, and weakened forces in Europe that wanted to intervene to help the Confederacy. Total abolition of slavery was finalized by the Thirteenth Amendment of 1865.

6. **Palmer raids**—After World War One and the Bolshevik Revolution in Russia, fear of communism was escalating in America. Everybody seemed to fear the so-called "Red Menace", a term introduced by Edgar J. Hoover. Partnering with Hoover was a man named A. Mitchell Palmer, US attorney general (1910—1921) notorious for the Palmer Raid — mass arrests of supposed subversives, many of whom were deported as aliens.

7. **McCarthyism**—McCarthy, Joseph Raymond, US Republican senator from Wis. (1947—1957) who created the "McCarthy era" in the mid-1950s through his sensational investigations into alleged communist subversion of American life. McCarthyism became a word for charges made without proof and accompanied by publicity.

Part I   Comprehension of the Text

1. What does it mean by "the paradox of patriotism"?
2. What had happened since the acts of war on Sept. 11 in United States?
3. What does it mean by "patriotism has almost always been at odds with itself" in Line 46?
4. In face of flag-fever, why do some other Americans feel coerced by patriotism?
5. According to the author, what should the American flag symbolize?

Part II   Vocabulary

A. Choose the one from the four choices that best explains the underlined word or phrase.

1. Forgetfulness can be frustrating and unnerving, so with this issue weighing heavily on her mind, she sets out to discover what midlife forgetfulness is all about.
   A. reassuring   B. reinvigorating   C. unsatisfying   D. discouraging

2. As the price of gold has skyrocketed, many fans have turned to jewelry pearl jewelry finished with high quality sterling silver.
   A. plunged sharply   B. increased rapidly   C. slumped greatly   D. descended quickly

3. Fill-in-the-blank, charts, word search and crosswords will reinforce vocabulary, writing and critical thinking skills.
   A. utilized   B. constrain   C. promote   D. strengthen

4. New media, such as blogs, Twitter, Facebook, and YouTube, have played a major role in episodes of contentious political action.
   A. controversial   B. ambiguous   C. suspicious   D. notorious

5. Filled with apprehension, she decides to see a psychiatrist and a neurologist and to get her brain scanned.
   A. remorse   B. despair   C. anxiety   D. sorrow

6. I often read about and hear about how designers must have the courage to speak truth to power and how political dissent is one pillar of patriotism.
   A. consensus   B. disagreement   C. divergence   D. uniformity

7. The historical context leading to Japanese <u>internment</u> can be illustrated in previous policies in the early 20th century toward Japanese immigrants.

  A. aggression   B. detention   C. captivation   D. restriction

8. They also make a powerful statement about human history and the struggle for human <u>emancipation</u> as a whole.

  A. liberation   B. cognition   C. equality   D. perfection

9. There was a need to develop more preventative rather than reactive strategies for combating abuse against women and children.

  A. segregation   B. corruption   C. discrimination   D. maltreatment

10. Such an accomplishment has <u>elevated</u> standards in the building and construction industry to create a worry-free basic building material for the public good.

  A. cultivated   B. activated   C. enhanced   D. created

B. Choose the one from the four choices that best completes the sentence.

1. A vast electronic spying operation has _____ computers and has stolen documents from hundreds of government and private offices around the world.

  A. infiltrated   B. permeated   C. penetrated   D. terminated

2. There are lots of angles to this story, beginning with simple truth that professional sports have _____ into something quite sad.

  A. involved   B. evolved   C. devolved   D. revolved

3. They must rely on information and advice provided by people whose interests may be considerably _____ with those of the company owners.

  A. on behalf   B. at odds   C. at stake   D. in contrast

4. A key area where cotton has _____ synthetics is in athletic wear, where popular performance fabrics have dented cotton's market share.

  A. taken place of   B. kept pace with   C. put emphasis on   D. lost ground to

5. The market was _____ between the bulls and the bears as the final trading day for this past week kicked off on Friday.

  A. weaving   B. wavering   C. wandering   D. waiving

6. In too many places around the world, the _____ of small arms and ammunition is a standing threat to the security of ordinary people.

  A. conservation   B. configuration   C. concession   D. proliferation

7. He is the greatest artist who has _____, in the sum of his works, the greatest number of the greatest ideas.

  A. empowered   B. embodied   C. motivated   D. anticipated

8. Charged with conspiring against the draft, they were convicted and sentenced to two years in prison with the possibility of _____ at the end of their term.

  A. exploitation   B. assimilation   C. deportation   D. assassination

9. Fire engine sirens _____ the normal sounds of Nairobi as they raced to battle a raging fire that claimed tens of lives.

A. filtered through　　B. turned away　　C. weighed down　　D. drowned out

10. The demonstration had been carefully stage-managed to _____ with the Prime Minister's visit.

　　A. coincide　　　　B. coordinate　　　　C. cooperate　　　　D. collaborate

C. Complete each sentence with the proper form of the word given in the parenthesis.

1. Many of the world's customs are not only harmless, but salutary, beautiful, _____, necessary to the very being of society. (noble)

2. Some of the genes _____ expressed in the HeLa cell cycle do not have a consistent correlation with tumor proliferation. (period)

3. Statements made during closing arguments do not amount to plain error unless they are determined to have had a _____ effect on the jury. (decide)

4. Only those young enough to be _____ by mortgages and other financial commitments are likely to continue spending freely. (burden)

5. The issue of _____ growth has been given top priority and in this direction, the banking sector is expected to play its part. (include)

6. Physical disabilities and _____ illness are considered to be in the medical domain and require the expertise of a physician. (system)

7. I have been involved in a large number of lawsuits, some of which are very significant and others which have been highly _____. (public)

8. The hybrids and their offspring should suffer no marked disturbance in their fertility in the _____ generations. (succeed)

9. The parliamentary committee on constitution amendment will recommend incorporating the _____ of independence into the constitution. (proclaim)

10. Acknowledging and allowing religious diversity is a necessary component of religious freedom and religious _____. (tolerate)

Part III　Cloze

Directions:There are totally 15 blanks in the following passage. Fill in each blank with the best one of the four options.

A problem with treating patriotism as an objective virtue is that patriotism often conflicts with other ideas. Soldiers of both sides in a war may feel ___1___ patriotic, creating an ethical ___2___. In his influential article "Is patriotism a virtue?" (1984) the philosopher Alasdair MacIntyre notes that most contemporary conceptions of morality ___3___ on a blindness to accidental traits such as local origin and ___4___ reject patriotic selectivity. MacIntyre constructs an alternative conception of morality that he claims would be ___5___ with patriotism.

Within nations, politicians may ___6___ to patriotic emotions in attacking their opponents, implicitly or explicitly ___7___ them of betraying the country. Minorities, on the other hand, may feel ___8___ from the political community and see no reason to be ___9___ of it and instead side with the group that most supports their ethnicity or religious belief.

Patriotism is often portrayed as a more positive   10   to nationalism, which sometimes carries   11   connotations. Some authors such as Morris Janowitz, Daniel Bar-Tal, or L. Snyder argue that patriotism is   12   from nationalism by its lack of aggression or   13   for others, its defensiveness, and positive community building. Others, such as Michael Billig or Jean Bethke Elshtain argue that the   14   is difficult to discern, and relies largely   15   the attitude of the labeler.

1. A. identically   B. conversely   C. equally   D. similarly
2. A. paradox   B. parameter   C. paradise   D. paradigm
3. A. persist   B. consist   C. resist   D. insist
4. A. nevertheless   B. therefore   C. furthermore   D. moreover
5. A. comparative   B. compared   C. compatible   D. comparing
6. A. appeal   B. contribute   C. adhere   D. conform
7. A. charging   B. converting   C. condemning   D. accusing
8. A. protected   B. excluded   C. sustained   D. restrained
9. A. content   B. familiar   C. proud   D. eager
10. A. alternative   B. alternate   C. altitude   D. alteration
11. A. negative   B. positive   C. formative   D. emotive
12. A. segregated   B. illuminated   C. interpreted   D. distinguished
13. A. loyalty   B. hatred   C. praise   D. respect
14. A. similarity   B. implication   C. difference   D. connotation
15. A. for   B. to   C. in   D. on

Part IV   Writing

Directions: Develop each of the following topics into an essay of about 200 words.

1. My Perspective on Patriotism
2. What factors increase the risk of terror? Think of social, economic and political aspects of the problems.
3. Construction of a Harmonious Society

Section B Extensive Reading and Translation

On Patriotism

By Ernest Partridge

[1] "Patriotism" is a word that has been hyper-conspicuous these days. The Congress of the United States has even chosen that word as a label for its anti-terrorism bill: "The USA PATRIOT Act".

[2] So just what does it mean to be a "patriot"? Who are today's "patriots"? What historical figures exemplify this civic virtue?

[3] And so, to begin, we ask: who was and is a "patriot"? Washington, Jefferson, Paine, those who pledged their lives, fortunes and sacred honor by

Patriotism

signing the Declaration of Independence—all these come to mind. But what about Colonel Klaus von Stauffenberg, whose failed attempt on Adolf Hitler's life cost the Colonel his life? Or Andrei Sakharov in the Soviet Union? More recently, how would we characterize John Dean during the Watergate affair? Or Daniel Ellsberg?

[4] The dominant meaning of "patriotism" as it is used today in the popular media seems to be "support of our nation's leadership during this time of peril". By implication, criticism of our leaders amounts to virtual treason.

[5] By this account, Washington, Jefferson, von Stauffenberg, Sakharov, and all those others mentioned above, were traitors, for they all rebelled against "constituted national leadership", i.e., King George (House of Hanover, not House of Bush), Adolf Hitler (legally elected Chancellor of Germany in 1933), the Brezhnev regime, and Richard Nixon, respectively.

[6] Clearly, unconditional allegiance to a leader will not do as a criterion of "patriotism". Otherwise, an "unpatriotic" or even "treasonous" leader would be an oxymoron. In fact, history provides an abundance of examples of such leaders. In our political tradition, it seems, "patriotism" implies a different object of loyalty than whosoever might, at the moment, be our appointed (or if we are lucky, our elected) leader.

[7] On reflection, it would seem that the "patriotism" exemplified by the founders of the American republic consists in an allegiance, not to persons, not to offices, and not even to institutions, but rather to political and moral ideals. Such ideals as self-determination, the social contract, inalienable human rights, and additional ideals such as those enumerated in the Declaration of Independence and the Bill of Rights.

[8] And yet, if polls and the pundits are to be believed, the prevailing public opinion demands that we accept without dissent and in the name of "patriotism", the legitimacy of an unelected

President, a curtailment of our liberties enumerated in the First, Fourth, Fifth and Sixth Amendments, which means our right to privacy, to *habeas corpus*, due process and competent counsel. In addition, the public appears willing to allow the President, through "executive order", to set aside acts of Congress, such as the Freedom of Information Act and the Presidential Records Act— in direct violation of the separation of powers stipulated by the Constitution.

[9] (1) Many brave individuals who have protested against such usurpations or who have criticized other aspects of the President's conduct in office have, if lucky, been met with scorn and derision from their fellow citizens, and if unlucky, they have lost their jobs. If recent history serves as a guide, there is no assurance that in the near future, still worse retaliation might await the dissenters.

[10] Clearly we seem to be dealing with two distinct and often conflicting concepts of patriotism. One is based upon a loyalty to individuals and offices, while the other is founded upon abstract moral and political *principles*.

[11] This distinction is illuminated by the work of two heavyweight Harvard professors: Moral philosopher, John Rawls, and the late cognitive psychologist, Lawrence Kohlberg. In independently developed yet remarkably similar theories, Rawls and Kohlberg describe "stages" of development of moral judgment and capacity. (2) As the individual matures and ascends to a higher stage of moral development, his judgment becomes more comprehensive, nuanced and integrated-more "cognitively adequate", to use Kohlberg's term. Moral puzzles that are insoluble on a "lower" level are resolved on a higher level. (e. g., should an impoverished husband steal a medicine to save the life of his desperately sick wife?)

[12] Kohlberg describes six stages of development, in three pairs: "pre-conventional" (obedience to authority), "conventional" (conformity to social norms), and "post-conventional" (moral autonomy—social contract in politics, and obedience to abstract principles in personal morality).

[13] Rawls's ascending categories are "Morality of Authority", "Morality of Association" and "Morality of Principles" (Theory of Justice, 1971, pp. 490-1). By this account, the child first develops a love and a loyalty to those most immediately and conveniently present and caring—his parents. The loyalty is extended to relatives and friends, and then to such abstractions as associations and institutions to which one's acquaintances (and oneself) belong. Finally, the loyalty attaches to the most abstract of entities, *ideals* and *principles*. A dramatic moral crisis, such as the Watergate Scandal, often illustrates the conflict between these three stages of morality. (3) In the Watergate affair, some officials were motivated by their loyalty to a person, i. e., Mr. Nixon. Others were moved by their loyalty to an institution, i. e., the Presidency. Still others, such as John Dean, acted in accordance with their duty to uphold the general principle of equal justice under the law.

[14] This conflict among concepts of "patriotism" as *obedience to authority*, as *conformity to convention* and as *loyalty to principle* resonates throughout history and literature. For example, Shakespeare thus depicts Brutus' justification of his assassination of Julius Caesar:

> Had you rather Caesar were living, and die all slaves, than that Caesar were dead, to live all free men? …Who is here so base that would be a bondman? Speak, for him have I offended

...Who is here so vile that will not love his country? Speak, for him have I offended.

[15] Anthony then turned the attention of the crowd toward Caesar's alleged personal virtues of charity, mercy, modesty and generosity (not conspicuous either in Shakespeare's portrayal or in historical accounts of Caesar's character). Anthony finally appeals to the greed of the crowd by producing a fraudulent "will" claiming to bequeath Caesar's fortune to the citizens. (Not unlike a promise of tax rebates.)

[16] Both appealed to "patriotism"—Brutus to a loyalty to principle, and Anthony to loyalty to a charismatic leader. The Roman mob chose Mark Anthony's lies and cult of personality over Brutus' ideals. And that decision marked the end of the Roman Republic.

[17] Today the American public may be facing a similar decision, and the predominant indications are that this public is more persuaded by Anthonian appeals to "stand behind our leader". And that is reason for grave concern.

[18] (4) If our republic is to endure, then any and all leaders and offices must be constrained by the principles of our Constitution and the rule of law, and must stand upon the foundation of the consent of the governed. That consent was violated in the disenfranchisement of the Florida voters before the 2000 election, by the harassment of election officials immediately following, and by the judicial *coup d'etat* by the Supreme Court in *Bush v. Gore*. The American public appears willing to "get over" this massive violation of the franchise. With this quasi-legitimacy safely in hand, the Bush Administration seems intent now upon dismantling the Constitutional system of checks and balances, along with the Bill of Rights.

[19] (5) If by "patriotism" we mean allegiance to shared political ideals, embodied in the rule of law, then a President and his Administration must earn the support of the public by exemplifying these ideals and by submitting to the constraints of the law and our national charter, The Constitution. After all, every President, in his very first act in office, takes an oath that he "will to the best of [his] ability, preserve, protect and defend the Constitution of the United States". That oath appears, *verbatim*, in the Constitution itself. (Article 2, Section 1)

[20] The President who fails to abide by this oath relinquishes his right to hold his office, and it becomes the patriotic duty of the legislature, the judiciary, and the citizenry to separate that President from his office.

[21] In the current controversy over "patriotism", our collective moral and political maturity is being severely tested, as we encounter this crucial question: "Is our ultimate loyalty to our leaders or to our Constitution?"

[22] The apparent answer of the American public today to that question must fill the authentic "patriot" with great concern—and greater resolution.

Part A　Translate English into Chinese

I. Translate the underlined sentences in the above text into Chinese.

II. Translate paragraphs 4, 5, 6 and 7 in the above text into Chinese.

Part B　Translate Chinese into English

I. Translate the following sentences into English with the words or phrases in the passage in Section B.

1. 一听到耐克,你就会想到运动员,就会想到其广告语"想做就做",这一现象正好例证了品牌的重要性。

2. 在那些能够理解毕加索的艺术的人看来,他属于那些启迪世界、帮助人们更清楚地理解生活的伟大艺术家的行列。

3. 毫无疑问,双方必须遵守已经同意并已签署过的合同条款。

4. 如果你拒绝我,我也只好接受现实,只得放手,因为那已是爱的尽头。

5. 独立生活的能力对于任何一个成年人来说都是必不可少的,但真正的成熟远远不只是一整套的生存策略。

II. Translate the following paragraph into English.

　　爱国主义是指个人和团体对自己的国家所持的一种积极和支持的态度。爱国主义包含了这样的态度:对祖国的成就和文化感到自豪;强烈希望保留祖国的特色和文化基础;对祖国其他同胞的认同感。爱国主义暗示着个体应将国家利益置于个人利益之上。爱国主义与民族主义有着紧密的联系,并通常被作为同义词使用。严格地说,民族主义是一种意识形态,强调一个人要忠于自己的国家,要以自己的国家为荣。民族主义可以说是爱国主义消极的一面。

Section A   Intensive Reading and Writing

Myth and Mythology

By Water Evans

[1] Put simply, a myth is a story that represents people's deepest feelings and experiences. Ancient or primitive people created myths to explain things which more sophisticated people explain through disciplines such as science, psychology, or theology. For example, a myth may explain a natural occurrence, such as the cycle of the seasons or the configuration of a constellation. Or it might embody a complicated human relationship, as between child and parent or man and woman. Or it might confront more metaphysical problems, such as the behavior of the gods, the role of Fate in a person's life, or what happens to one after death. Thus, David Leeming has described myth as "the metaphorical, symbolical, or direct expression of the 'unknown'".

[2] Several misconceptions about myth need to be dispelled. One is that myths were the exclusive property of the ancient Greeks and Romans. Though we are perhaps most familiar with Greek and Roman mythology, myths are common to all people, in all times, throughout the world.

[3] Another misconception, this one more serious, is that myths are "fairytales", stories which have no basis in fact and hence may be discredited. Nothing could be further from the truth. Rather than being falsehoods, myths are the essence of truth, a reflection of humanity's universal experience, enduring out-side the limitations of time and place. Scratch the surface of any myth and you'll discover its essential truth. Akin to the notion that myths are un-truth is the belief that we have "out-grown" the need for myths, that they are a kind of fossilized remains of ancient civilizations, interesting perhaps to a few specialists but of little value to an advanced technological society. On the contrary, myth is basic to human existence as we know it. It is as real as human concerns are real. When we lose our ability to respond to and appreciate the mythic element, we are in grave danger of

becoming automatons, of losing that which makes us uniquely and truly human. Indeed, the society which has lost its mythic sensibility may be said to have lost its soul.

[4] Let us look more closely at myths to see why this is true. For one thing, myths, like dreams, serve as psychic escape valves. Indeed, myths have been called racial dreams. Most of us have had dreams in which we were being chased, and managed to escape, in which we were engaged in some contest that we won (or lost), in which we were looking for something of great value, or in which we encountered something that endangered our lives. Similarly, most societies have myths which express on a group level the same fears or wishes which dreams express for the individual. And just as an individual may become psychotic if deprived of dream producing sleep, so a society which has lost its myth-making ability may drift toward self-destruction.

[5] Buried deep within our individual unconscious lies what has been called our "collective unconscious" or racial memory: a vague sense of familiarity with certain events that we have not personally experienced. Although psychologists disagree as to the origin or cause of this phenomenon, it is true that we respond emotionally when presented with certain themes, images, or patterns of action. These themes—called archetypes—seem to "strike a chord" of recognition whenever we encounter them. Fairy tales, folk legends, fantasies, as well as great works of literature often employ archetypes. Unless we have been trained to look for them, however, we usually are not aware of their presence; we simply know that we "like the work and seem emotionally drawn to it". (The popularity of certain movies like Star Wars or the writings of J. R. R. Tolkein may in part be attributed to their incorporation of archetypal themes.) Since virtually all myths present us with archetypes of one form or another, we see once again the relevance of myth to our everyday lives.

[6] We may now turn from the general to the specific and examine a particular pattern that is perhaps the most basic and most common of all archetypes. This pattern is called the "monomyth" because it reflects the single, essential, most inclusive pattern of human experience. The nuclear unit of the monomyth may be expressed by the formula of separation, initiation, and return. Epic heroes such as Odysseus, Aeneas, and Dante all follow this pattern. Moreover, our own lives if we examine them closely usually resemble the monomythic pattern in whole or in part. (We leave the familiarity of home and go away, to college, to a big city, to war, and eventually return, changed by our experience.) Thus the pattern of the individual life merges with the universal myth.

[7] While our own lives may partake of the monomyth, it is the hero who best expresses the archetypal adventurer in his journey through life and beyond. Joseph Campbell describes the mythic hero as that individual who is able to return from his adventure with "the power to bestow boons on his fellow man". The journey of the hero may be divided into eight stages, which are the supreme mythic events in the life of the hero and which correspond on a psychological level to certain significant periods in the development of each individual. The first such event is birth, and while each of us begins our life by being born, the hero's birth is generally miraculous or unusual in the extreme. He or she may be the product of a miraculous conception resulting from the union of a mortal and divine being, like the birth of Helen after Zeus disguised as a swan raped Leda. Or, he may have undergone some singular experience shortly after birth, such as being lost or abandoned by his natural parents and suckled by beasts, as in the case of Romulus, or rescued and adopted, like Oedipus. The second

stage, childhood and adolescence, also is marked by up usual events. The hero may be precociously strong or intelligent, amazing his elders with feats of strength or great wisdom. Frequently, also, his acts are marked by a divine sign proclaiming his special nature. Or if the hero is more "normal" in terms of his own strength and skill, he may have special "protectors" or talismans which give him assistance along the way. At any rate, childhood is a first stage of initiation in which the child must confront and master a superior force or receive the psychic reassurance that he needs to move on to the next stage.

[8] Once he has successfully passed through the initiation stage, the hero then withdraws for a period of time in preparation for the next, active phase. His withdrawal stage is usually one of meditation and passivity, a looking into the self and achieving an awareness of one's unique identity or mission. Paradoxically, the hero must lose himself in order to find himself. Then, gathering his psychic powers he is ready to return to the world to undertake his great tasks. Frequently, the hero is tempted during his withdrawal by a representative of "the world", usually a devil-figure. This is particularly true in the case of saints (like Saint Anthony) or religious figures (like Jesus and Buddha). In classical myth the withdrawal may take the form of the descent into the underworld, symbolically an exploration of the hidden recesses of the psyche. For example, it has been pointed out that Odysseus' descent to the underworld in Book XI of the Odyssey is unnecessary in terms of the action of the poem; for once, the hero does nothing; he merely sees and questions, and the instructions given him by Tiresias are less explicit than those supplied by Kirke later on. But Odysseus needs the vision the underworld offers him; he must confront his past—his mother, his comrades in arms who died at Troy—before he can face the future—the killing of the suitors. The same might be said for Aeneas, who must envision the future glory of Rome in the underworld before he is ready to endure the hardships of war and colonization.

[9] The fourth stage involves labor or quest. This represents the active period of full maturity. In this stage the hero does great deeds, like Hercules, Achilles, Theseus; or he goes on a journey— like Odysseus, Sinbad, Jason. He must confront and overcome the external forces in life as he did the internal forces in the previous stage. The fourth stage is ended by the fifth stage: death. One might think that this would end the process altogether, but for the mythic hero, death, like birth, is extraordinary. In a sense, his labors of stage four simply continue into stage five, for here he must confront physical death—the greatest foe of all. The mythic hero thus becomes the scapegoat, enduring death for all men. In vicariously experiencing his death, we die also, and so psychologically he relieves us of our fear and anxiety. His death is often terrible in the extreme, involving great suffering or the total destruction of the body and its life-giving properties; often he is dismembered or castrated. In stage six the hero continues in his role as quester and scapegoat as he descends to the underworld. Psychologically, he represents the desire of each of us to penetrate the mystery of death and understand it. He must struggle with the forces of death and overcome them. Paradoxically, the descent into the underworld holds the promise of renewed life; death and fertility are inseparable in nature, and so in the myth death is followed by re-birth. The seventh step, then, is resurrection, the return of the hero from the underworld. Again, psychologically he represents our desire to overcome and as he triumphs, so vicariously do we. The hero, however, is extraordinary in that he brings with

him a gift, a knowledge, a "boon" which he can share with others and which has far-reaching effects. His adventure brings about a change in the lives of many. Thus in the final stage the true uniqueness of the hero is made manifest. He transcends his role as "Everyman", as humanity's representative, and becomes more than human; that is, he becomes divine. He ascends to heaven and achieves union with the mother-goddess, atonement with the father-creator, or apotheosis, becoming himself a god. We may explain this final step psychologically by saying that the human being, having dealt with the problems of birth, childhood, adolescence, and maturity, having faced the internal and external trials of existence, turns at last to confront the mystery of the unknown.

[10] Mythology, because it expresses the basic drives, fears, and longings of humankind, is of crucial importance. As Carl Jung wrote, "it is possible to live the fullest life only when we are in harmony with these symbols; wisdom is a return to them. It is a question neither of belief nor knowledge, but of the agreement of our thinking with the primordial images of the unconscious".

Notes to the Text

1. **Leeming, David Adams**—the author of "Mythology: The Voyage of the Hero".
2. **Odysseus**—a king of Ithaca and Greek leader in the Trojan War who after the war wanders 10 years before reaching home.
3. **Aeneas**—a son of Anchises and Aphrodite, defender of Troy, and hero of Vergil's Aeneid.
4. **Joseph Campbell**(March 26, 1904-October 30, 1987)—an American mythologist, writer and lecturer, best known for his work in comparative mythology and comparative religion. His work is vast, covering many aspects of the human experience. His philosophy is often summarized by his phrase: "Follow your bliss". Campbell's term **monomyth**, also referred to as **the hero's journey**, refers to a basic pattern found in many narratives from around the world. This widely distributed pattern was first fully described in *The Hero with a Thousand Faces* (1949).
5. **Helen**—the wife of Menelaus, famous for her beauty. According to legend her abduction by Paris brought about the Trojan War.
6. **Zeus**—the supreme god, identified with the Latin Jupiter. He was the son of Rhea and of Cronos, whom he overthrew. He symbolized nature and the elements and was regarded variously as the god of the earth and giver of fertility, the dispenser of good and evil, the giver of laws, the guardian of the hearth, property and liberty. His symbols were the eagle, the scepter and the thunderbolt, and his principal shrines were in Athens and Olympia.
7. **Leda**—the wife of a king of Sparta. She was loved by Zeus, who came to her in the form of a swan. She was the mother of Castor, Pollux, Helen and Clytemnestra.
8. **Romulus**—one of the twin sons of Mars. He was exposed in infancy, but were suckled by a she-wolf and then brought up by a shepherd. According to tradition, Romulus was the founder of Rome (753 B.C.).
9. **Oedipus**—the son of Lairs, king of Thebes, and Jocasta. Because of the oracle that he would kill his father and marry his mother, he was left on a hillside, but was rescued and brought up as the son of the king of Corinth. Hearing the oracle, Oedipus left Corinth. While traveling he met and

killed Laius, without recognizing him. After ridding Thebes of the Sphinx. He married Jocasta and became king, unwittingly fulfilling the oracle. Later realizing the truth of his birth, he stabbed out his eyes and went into exile with his daughter Antigone as guide. His story was used by Sophocles in "Oedipus Rex" and "Oedipus at Colonus".

10. **Saint Anthony** (of Egypt c: 251—356)—Christian hermit in the deserts of Egypt who is regarded as the father of monasticism.

11. **Jesus** (c. 6 B.C.—30 A.D.)—a Jewish religious leader whom Christians worship as the Son of God and Saviour of Mankind, the Christ. His life, teaching, death and resurrection are described in the Gospels of the New Testment, while the Epistles supply other details. Jesus was the won of Nary, wife of Joseph, a carpenter of Nazareth, and they were in Bethlehem at the time of the birth because a census was being taken. According to the gospel Nary was his only human parent (Virgin Birth).

12. **Buddha** (563—483 B.C.)—the Indian founder of Buddhism, son of Gautama a nobleman and member of the Kshatriya caste.

13. **Tiresias** (Gk mythol)—a blind prophet of Thebes mentiooooned frequently in Greek literature, esp. in connection with the family of Oedipus.

14. **troy**—an ancient city (Trojan War) near the western entrance to the Dardenelles. In modern Turkey.

15. **Hercules**—a demigod identified with Heracles.

16. **Achilles**—son of the Phthian king Peleus and the sea-goddess Thetis, who plunged him into the Styx so as to make him invulnerable (except for the heel by which she held him).

17. **Theseus**—hero and king of Athens.

18. **Jason**—a legendary Greeek hro distinguished for his successful quest of the Golden Fleece; a prince who led the Argonauts to win the Golden Fleece with the aid of Medea.

19. **Carl Gustav Jung** (26 July 1875—6 June 1961)—a Swiss psychiatrist, an influential thinker and the founder of Analytical Psychology. Jung is often considered the first modern psychologist to state that the human psyche is "by nature religious" and to explore it in depth. Many pioneering psychological concepts were originally proposed by Jung, including the Archetype, the Collective Unconscious, the Complex, and synchronicity.

Part I Comprehension of the Text

1. What is "myth"? What is "mythology"?
2. According to the author, what misconceptions about myth are there in the world public?
3. Why is myth basic to human existence?
4. What is "individual unconscious"? What is "collective unconscious"?
5. What is "monomyth"? And what does it consist of?
6. What are the stages that the mythic hero usually goes through?

Part II Vocabulary

A. Choose the one from the four choices that best explains the underlined word or phrase.

1. Another common <u>misconception</u> is that if women do a lot of fitness training and weights, their body becomes uptight and stiff.

   A. mistaken notion   B. false opinion   C. popular idea   D. valid belief

2. The proof that the <u>resurrection</u> of Jesus Christ actually occurred as a historical event is established by numerous supporting facts or evidences.

   A. recovery   B. rebirth   C. uprising   D. ascent

3. After spotting dozens of planets in exotic orbits, scientists have found a planetary system that <u>resembles</u> our solar system.

   A. looks about   B. looks after   C. looks over   D. looks like

4. As the world advances through the information age we must <u>envision</u> harmony and leave a better world for the children of our children.

   A. visualize   B. supervise   C. conceive   D. actualize

5. The local government has approved of a proposal to introduce <u>sophisticated</u> techniques to promote economic growth.

   A. important   B. difficult   C. advanced   D. scientific

6. The size and <u>configuration</u> of a site and any accessible adjacent properties can have a major impact on the kinds of recreational use it can support.

   A. nature   B. shape   C. bulk   D. size

7. He suggests that if you <u>scratch the surface of</u> most human-generated disasters, you find something else at play: pride, arrogance, and indolence.

   A. dip into   B. think about   C. make out   D. focus on

8. A group of scientists believe they have finally <u>dispelled</u> the myth that eating late at night causes weight gain.

   A. abolished   B. confirmed   C. removed   D. justified

9. His study in the medical journal was widely <u>discredited</u> after Britain's medical regulator found it did not meet ethical standards.

   A. disavowed   B. debated   C. refuted   D. disbelieved

10. The Brooklyn Bridge was the <u>archetype</u> of the many spans that now connect Manhattan with Long Island and New Jersey.

    A. original model   B. specific example   C. typical design   D. unique device

B. Choose the one from the four choices that best completes the sentence.

1. Once your doctor confirms that your child has _____ the milk allergy, make sure to follow his recommendations as to how to introduce dairy foods back into the diet.

   A. overwhelmed   B. withstood   C. overturned   D. outgrown

2. Their growth and success is _____ to the innovation and commitment of the members and the Gloucester community.

A. distributed   B. attributed   C. contributed   D. accustomed

3. They felt that the hard things which I said to her were only superficial, and that I should be unable to resist the first smile which she might _____ upon me.

     A. bestow   B. impose   C. inflict   D. embark

4. This feeling of _____ and comfort applies particularly to the wiring and plumbing systems which will be brand new in new homes.

     A. ignorance   B. arrogance   C. reassurance   D. acquaintance

5. Relaxation through _____ is one of the most effective ways to beat stress and is extremely simple to master.

     A. meditation   B. medication   C. mediation   D. medicament

6. Truth may be stretched, but cannot be broken, and always gets above _____, as does oil above water.

     A. likelihood   B. falsehood   C. stupidity   D. ridicule

7. In the wake of the country legalizing both the use of marijuana, and gay marriage, many people seek a safe place to _____ of these new liberties.

     A. participate   B. particularize   C. partake   D. patronize

8. Several futurists argue that artificial intelligence will _____ the limits of progress and fundamentally transform humanity.

     A. descend   B. transcend   C. ascend   D. transcribe

9. When wholeness exists, and each of its elements is working in _____ with the others, a balance is created that allows the body to heal itself.

     A. harmony   B. consistence   C. accordance   D. conjunction

10. Education for all is the slogan goal and objective in the modern times, then why should women be _____ of learning to read and write?

     A. dispersed   B. depressed   C. despaired   D. deprived

C. Complete each sentence with the proper form of the word given in the parenthesis.

1. A team of researchers have discovered _____ feathers from a giant penguin that lived near the Equator more than 36 million years ago. (fossil)

2. We've all read news stories and seen documentaries that describe the numbers of animal and plant species that are now _____ or extinct. (danger)

3. Grass-root sport enjoys great _____ in China, with more than 300 million people participating in sports exercise regularly. (popular)

4. With each passing year, the young Albert Einstein's achievements in physics in the year 1905 seem to be ever more _____. (miracle)

5. When a medication is stopped, _____ from the drug results in a return to the original symptom, often in a much worse state. (withdraw)

6. With the development of the Games throughout the 20th century, the five rings and the flag have become _____ from the Olympic Movement and the Olympic Games. (separate)

7. Researchers used advanced imaging to chart brain _____ based on the functional connections between brain regions. (mature)

8. In a groundbreaking new book, Harvard researchers look at the role of diet, exercise and weight control in _____. (fertile)

9. _____ speaking, the attempt to understand another often has the opposite effect of creating mutual hostility. (paradox)

10. As we increase the body of information surrounding a specific aspect of the future, we increase our _____ with it. (familiar)

Part III Cloze

Directions: There are totally 15 blanks in the following passage. Fill each blank with one word only.

Why study The Hero's Journey? Why learn a pattern that dates from before recorded history? The answer is simple: we should study it __1__ it's the pattern of human experience, of our experience. We live it now, and we will live it for the rest of our lives.

__2__, every challenge or change we face in life is a journey. Every love found, every love __3__, every birth and every death carries the potential of __4__ to a new level of understanding. Every move to a new school, job, or city __5__ the chance to stop being what we were and to __6__ being what we can become. Every situation which __7__ us with something new or which forces us to re-evaluate our thinking, behavior or perspective presents us __8__ possibilities for insight and growth.

The journey is a process of self-discovery and self-integration, of __9__ balance and harmony in our lives. As with any process of growth and change, a journey can be __10__ and painful, but it brings __11__ to develop confidence, perspective and a new way of being in our world.

Understanding the Journey pattern can help us understand the literature we read, the movies we see, and the experiences which __12__ our life. By recognizing the Journey's stages and __13__ they function, we will develop a sense of the flow of our own experience and be __14__ able to make decisions and solve problems. More __15__, we will begin to recognize our own points of passage and respect the significance they have for us.

1. A. if   B. because   C. when   D. though
2. A. In a word   B. To an extent   C. As a whole   D. In a sense
3. A. lost   B. given   C. felt   D. made
4. A. contribution   B. concentration   C. transformation   D. transaction
5. A. opens   B. reduces   C. takes   D. stands
6. A. enjoy   B. mind   C. avoid   D. start
7. A. accustoms   B. confronts   C. acquaints   D. conforms
8. A. to   B. for   C. with   D. /
9. A. maintaining   B. entertaining   C. sustaining   D. restraining

10. A. pleasing   B. surprising   C. exciting   D. confusing

11. A. prerequisites   B. opportunities   C. presumptions   D. suppositions

12. A. improve   B. attract   C. shape   D. affect

13. A. why   B. when   C. that   D. how

14. A. better   B. further   C. rather   D. quite

15. A. essentially   B. importantly   C. differently   D. necessarily

Part IV　Writing

Directions: Develop each of the following topics into an essay of about 200 words.

1. As expressed in the reading passage, "our own lives if we examine them closely usually resemble the monomythic pattern in whole or in part". Interpret the term "monomyth" with your own life experience.

2. Myths are common to all people, in all times, throughout the world. Do you agree? Explain.

3. Use the theory of Hero's Journey to analyze a film you're most familiar with.

Section B   Extensive Reading and Translation

The Power of Myth

By Dwight Longenecker

[1] One of the most influential forces in American cinema of the second half of the twentieth century is a man who was not a film maker at all. The self styled 'mythologist' Joseph Campbell, became a mentor for the new breed of film makers of the 1970s. John Boorman and Francis Copolla have acknowledged their debt to his work. His influences are seen in the work of Steven Spielberg, and most especially in the films of George Lucas, the creator of Star Wars. Lucas was actually friends with Campbell, and admits that Campbell's writings helped him structure his famous inter-galactic fantasy saga.

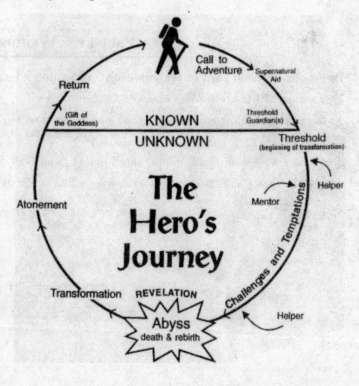

[2] In his seminal work, The Hero with a Thousand Faces, Campbell outlined the essential structure at the heart of all the world's great stories. Having studied James Joyce's Finnegan's Wake, Campbell borrowed the term "monomyth" and expanded the concept to illustrate how the structure of the hero's quest undergirds the world's myths, legends and folk tales. (1) The "monomyth" is very simple: in Campbell's words, "The hero ventures forth from a world of common day into a region of supernatural wonder: fabulous forces are there encountered, and a decisive victory is won. The hero comes back from this mysterious adventure with the power to bestow boons on his fellow man. "

[3] Campbell broke this basic structure down into twenty or so stages. (2) He believed that the hero's quest is not only the root structure of all great stories, but it was so because the hero's quest is the basic structure for life's adventure. He thought the quest-based story structure was universal because it represented not only the dynamic of the human life cycle, but also the more important cycle of inner development and spiritual growth. The adventure was not only to be an outward quest, but an inner one. In fact, Campbell taught, it is the inner growth of the hero that is most important to the telling of the tale. Campbell said, "it is the business of mythology proper, and of the fairy tale, to reveal the specific dangers and techniques of the dark interior way...the passage of the hero may be

over ground incidentally; fundamentally it is inward".

[4] By the 1970's film makers were at a crossing point. Like most art forms, film had grown organically according to the demands of the marketplace. At first there was no particular theory, and creative writers and directors developed a visual method for story telling by trial and error. The successful film directors and screenwriters had an instinct for a good story, but there was very little to help writers analyse what made a story work. Christopher Vogler was working for the Disney studios when he came across Campbell's work. He wrote a little booklet to guide story editors, and from that work came his now classic guide to screenwriting, The Writer's Journey. Vogler acknowledges his debt to Campbell and believes that Campbell's work has provided a basic template for all screenwriters.

[5] As a result, most mainstream Hollywood films now follow the structure of the hero's myth at least in part. Early in the film the audience is introduced to the Hero's "Ordinary World". The hero then experiences some sort of "Call to Adventure". He refuses the call, meets a mentor and then embarks on the adventure. The outward journey goes through several other stages before the predicted resolution as the hero claims the prize and then returns with the great boon for the redemption and good of his old world, and the people in it.

[6] If the formula is followed slavishly the result is an exciting, but predictable blockbuster. The same stock characters show up. The plot follows the same turning points, and even the "twists" in the plot turn out to be predictable. This is not always a bad thing. Very often an audience enjoys an adventure film because there is an element of predictability about it. The expected form becomes a language of its own and the audience knows what to expect and enjoys the result just as much as a reader looks forward to their favourite mystery writer's annual offering.

[7] While this hero's quest provides a template which is sometimes formulaic, the good screenwriter is always able to use the structure to surprise the audience, genuinely turn the plot and carry the audience into a new understanding of reality. At the same time, the good screenwriter and director are aware of the deeper aspects of good story-telling, and they use the emotional turning points of the plot to engage their audience in moral choices and spiritually positive decisions.

[8] (3) Joseph Campbell was a great believer in the power of myth, and believed that the mysterious language, symbols and plot lines in mythic literature connected humanity with the deep movements of the human psyche within the collective unconscious. Brought up as a Catholic in New York City, Campbell was entranced by the beauty and mystical quality of Catholic worship. He was also fascinated by the folktales and culture of Native Americans. As he grew older, Campbell drifted from the Catholic faith. He was dismayed by the results of the second Vatican Council, believing that the Church had sold her patrimony. He relished the mystery of the ancient Mass with its rich symbolism and multi-layered rituals and meaning. He thought the Catholic Church had got rid of the only thing it was good at to turn her liturgy into a string of banal greeting card sentiments, and her clergy into social workers. Campbell's own end point was a mish mash of New Age beliefs. Basically syncretistic and agnostic, he relied heavily on the work of Carl Jung, and believed that salvation lay within psychology and self help.

[9] Joseph Campbell's work has been picked up by all the usual New Age suspects. With its

mix of shallow mysticism, depth psychology and self help, it offers an intriguing matrix with which to view the world. However, without genuine faith, mysticism and the work of grace, Campbell's thought (like all New Age prognostications and therapies) remains an interesting theory.

[10] Nevertheless, although in his public expression Joseph Campbell left the Catholic faith, it can be argued that the Catholic faith didn't leave him. The Catholic religion was Campbell's first (and arguably) deepest inspiration and it provided the initial driving force for his search for truth within the stories of mankind. (4) <u>Since Campbell has been so influential in the popular culture of our time, it is worth remembering that while he cannot be called a 'Catholic thinker', the roots of his thought and his search for truth are locked deep within his Catholic boyhood, and his basic insights can help illuminate our understanding of stories, film and literature.</u>

[11] How very deep that faith was within Campbell is proved by the story I heard when conducting a seminar on preaching in Vermont. I mentioned Campbell's work in the context of structuring stories for use in homilies. A participant on the course was a deacon who was, for many years, a professor of phenomenology and religious psychology. He had met Campbell several times and was a student of the religious philosopher Mircea Eleade. The deacon told me that on his deathbed Joseph Campbell was received back into communion with the Catholic faith.

[12] The essence of Campbell's work is his analysis of the structure of stories. The hero launches out from his ordinary world to gain a great treasure, but he always returns. If it is true that Campbell returned to the Catholic faith, then his own life went through a similar cycle. He went away from the church, and returned, bringing with him a new understanding of the 'monomyth' and how it works within the human heart. (5) <u>Perhaps he came 'home to Rome' with a fresh way to appreciate not only the world's great stories, but also the great Judeo-Christian story which culminates in the greatest story ever told—the story of Christ's own heroic descent to this world to win the prize of mankind's salvation.</u> As C. S. Lewis observed, "This was a myth that really happened". By showing us how myth works Campbell unlocks another dimension of our own redemption.

Part A   Translate English into Chinese

I. Translate the underlined sentences in the above text into Chinese.

II. Translate paragraphs 5, 6 and 7 in the above text into Chinese.

Part B   Translate Chinese into English

I. Translate the following sentences into English with the words or phrases in the passage in Section B.

1. 植物根部将从泥土或叶子中吸收来的化学物质进行分解,使其转变成营养。

2. 准确报道死亡矿工的人数不仅是尊重这些生命的价值,而且能防止类似悲剧再次发生。

3. 我国经济体制的全面改革刚刚起步,总的方向、原则有了,具体章法还要在试验中一步步立起来。

4. 我们在实行这个计划时必然会遇到困难,但我们有决心把它们一一克服。

5. 对违法犯罪的未成年人,实行教育、感化、挽救的方针,坚持教育为主、惩罚为辅的原则。

II. Translate the following paragraphs into English.

　　由于原型心理学的出现,人们有可能了解神话的本质与作用,而不致有因为理性主义或浪漫主义而排斥神话的危险。这是因为首先人们可以想象原型的本质,它首先以形象出现,而且将原型心理学的全过程看作是一种方法是富于想象的,由此我进一步认为形象不是我所看到的,而是我是怎么看的。

　　这种想法/看法使我将形象看成心灵的活动,因此,使我接受这样的观念:思想寓于想象而非想象寓于思想。这种逻辑的巧妙变化反映了对神话的理解,使我开阔了眼界,不再暗地认为神话不存在。

Section A   Intensive Reading and Writing

The City

By John V. Lindsay

[1] In one sense, we can trace all the problems of the American city back to a single starting point: we Americans don't like our cities very much.

[2] That is, on the face of it, absurd. After all, more than three-fourths of us now live in cities, and more are flocking to them every year. We are told that the problems of our cities are receiving more attention in Washington, and scholarship has discovered a whole new field in urban studies.

[3] Nonetheless, it is historically true; in the American psychology, the city has been a basically suspect institution, filled with the corruption of Europe, totally lacking that sense of spaciousness and innocence of the frontier and the rural landscape.

[4] I don't pretend to be a scholar on the history of the city in American life. But my thirteen years in public office, first as an officer of the U. S. Department of Justice[1], then as Congressman, and now as Mayor of the biggest city in America, have taught me all too well that fact that a strong anti-urban attitude runs consistently through the mainstream of American thinking. Much of the drive behind the settlement of America was in reaction to the conditions in European industrial centers—and much of the theory supporting the basis of freedom in America was linked directly to the availability of land and the perfectibility of man outside the corrupt influences of the city.

[5] What has this to do with the predicament of the modern city? I think it has much to do with

it. For the fact is that the United States, particularly the federal government, which has historically established our national priorities, has simply never thought that the American city was "worthy" of improvement—at least not to the extent of expending any basic resources on it.

[6] Antipathy to the city predates the American experience. When industrialization drove the European working man into the major cities of the continent, books and pamphlets appeared attacking the city as a source of crime, corruption, filth, disease, vice, licentiousness, subversion, and high prices. The theme of some of the earliest English novels—Moll Flamders[2], for example—is that of the innocent country youth coming to the big city and being subjected to al forms of horror until justice— and a return to the pastoral life—follow.

[7] The proper opinion of Europe seemed to support the Frenchman who wrote: "In the country, a man's mind is free and easy...; but in the city, the persons of friends and acquaintances, one's own and other people's business, foolish quarrels, ceremonies, visits, impertinent discourses, and a thousand other fopperies and diversions steal away the greatest part of our time and leave no leisure for better and necessary employment. Great towns are but a larger sort of prison to the soul, like cages to birds or pounds to beasts".

[8] This was not, of course, the only opinion on city life. Others maintained that the city was "the fireplace of civilization, whence light and heat radiated out into the cold dark world". And William Penn[3] planned Philadelphia as the "holy city", carefully laid out so that each house would have the appearance of a country cottage to avoid the density and overcrowding that so characterized European cities.

[9] Without questions, however, the first major thinker to express a clear antipathy to the urban way of life was Thomas Jefferson[4]. For Jefferson, the political despotism of Europe and the economic despotism of great concentrations of wealth, on the one hand, and poverty on the other, were symbolized by the cities of London and Paris, which he visited frequently during his years as a diplomatic representative of the new nation. In the new world, with its opportunities for widespread landholding, there was the chance for a flowering of authentic freedom, with each citizen, freed from economic dependence, both able and eager to participate in charging the course of his own future. America, in a real sense, was an escape from all the injustice that had flourished in Europe— injustice that was characterized by the big city.

[10] This Jeffersonian theme was to remain an integral part of the American tradition. Throughout the nineteenth century, as the explorations of America pushed farther outward, the new settlers sounded most like each other in their common celebration of freedom from city chains.

[11] The point is that all this opinion goes beyond ill feelings; it suggests a strong national sense that encouragement and development of the city was to be in no sense a national priority—that our manifest destiny[5] lay in the untouched lands to the west, in constant movement westward, and in maximum dispersion of land to as many people as possible.

[12] Thus, the Northwest Ordinance of 1787[6]—perhaps the first important declaration of national policy—explicitly encouraged migration into the Northwest Territory and provided grants of land and free public lands for schools. New York City, by contrast, did not begin a public-education system until 1892—and received, of course, no federal help at all. Similarly, the Homestead Act of

1862[7] based on an assumption—supported by generations of American theory—that in the West could be found genuine opportunity and that the eastern-seaboard cities of the United States were simply hopeless collections of vice and deprivation.

[13] This belief accelerated after the Civil War, for a variety of reasons. For one thing, the first waves of immigration were being felt around the country as immigrants arrived in urban areas. The poverty of the immigrants, largely from Ireland and Northern Europe, caused many people in rural America to equate poverty with personal inferiority—a point of view that has not yet disappeared from our national thinking. Attacks on the un-American and criminal tendencies of the Irish, the Slavs[8], and every other ethnic group that arrived on America's shore were a steady part of national thinking, as were persistent efforts to bar any further migration of "undesirables" to our country.

[14] With the coming rapid industrialization, all the results of investigations into city poverty and despair that we think of as recent findings were being reported—and each report served to confirm the beliefs of the Founding Fathers that the city was no place for a respectable America.

[15] Is all this relevant only to past attitudes and past legislative history? I don't think so. The fact is that until today, this same basic belief—that our cities ought to be left to fend for themselves— is still a powerful element in our national tradition.

[16] Consider more modern history. The most important housing act in the last twenty-five years was not the law that provided for public housing; it was the law that permitted the Federal Housing Administration (FHA)[9] to grant subsidized low-interest mortgages to Americans who want to purchase homes. More than anything else, this has made the suburban dream a reality. It has brought the vision of grass, trees, and a place for the kids to play within the reach of millions of working Americans, and the consequences be damned. The impact of such legislation on the cities was not even considered—nor was the concept of making subsidized money available for neighborhood renovation in the city so that it might compete with the suburbs. Instead, in little more than a decade 800,000 middle income New Yorkers fled the city for the suburbs and were replaced by largely unskilled workers who in many instances represented a further cost rather than an economic asset.

[17] And it was not a hundred years ago but two years ago that a suggested law giving a small amount of federal money for rat control was literally laughed off the floor of the House of Representatives amid much joking about discrimination against country rats in favor of city rats.

[18] What happened, I think, was not the direct result of a "the city is evil and therefore we will not help it" concept. It was more indirect, more subtle, the result of the kind of thinking that enabled us to spend billions of dollars in subsidies to preserve the family farm while doing nothing about an effective program for jobs in the city; to create government agencies concerned with the interests of agriculture, veterans, small business, labor, commerce, and the American Indian but to create no Department of Urban Development[10] until 1965; to so restrict money that meaningful federal aid is still not possible.

[19] In other words, the world of urban America as dark and desolate place undeserving of support or help has become fixed in the American consciousness. And we are paying for that attitude in our cities today.

Notes to the Text

1. **U. S. Department of Justice**—美国司法部 often referred to as the **Justice Department** or **DOJ**. It is the United States federal executive department responsible for the enforcement of the law and administration of justice, equivalent to the justice or interior ministries of other countries.

2. *Moll Flanders*—a novel written by Daniel Defoe in 1722, after his work as a journalist and pamphleteer. By 1722, Defoe had become a recognised novelist, with the success of *Robinson Crusoe* in 1719.

3. **William Penn** (1644—1718)—an English real estate entrepreneur, philosopher, and founder and "absolute proprietor" of the Province of Pennsylvania, the English North American colony and the future Commonwealth of Pennsylvania. He was an early champion of democracy and religious freedom, notable for his good relations and successful treaties with the Lenape Indians. Under his direction, the city of Philadelphia was planned and developed.

4. **Thomas Jefferson** (1743—1826)—the third President of the United States (1801—1809) and the principal author of the Declaration of Independence (1776). An influential Founding Father, Jefferson envisioned America as a great "Empire of Liberty" that would promote republicanism.

5. **Manifest Destiny**—the 19th century American belief that the United States was destined to expand across the North American continent, from the Atlantic Seaboard to the Pacific Ocean. It was used by Democrats in the 1840s to justify the war with Mexico; the concept was denounced by Whigs, and fell into disuse after the mid-19th century.

6. **The Northwest Ordinance**—formally An Ordinance for the Government of the Territory of the United States, North-West of the River Ohio, and also known as the Freedom Ordinance or "The Ordinance of 1787", an act of the Congress of the Confederation of the United States, passed July 13, 1787. The primary effect of the ordinance was the creation of the Northwest Territory as the first organized territory of the United States out of the region south of the Great Lakes, north and west of the Ohio River, and east of the Mississippi River.

7. **The Homestead Act of 1862**—a law which gave a 160-acre piece of land to anyone who lived on it for 5 years.

8. **Slaves**—members of a race spread over most of Eastern Europe, including Poles, Russians, Bulgarians, etc.

9. **Federal Housing Administration** (**FHA**)—a United States government agency created as part of the National Housing Act of 1934. It insured loans made by banks and other private lenders for home building and home buying. The goals of this organization are to improve housing standards and conditions, provide an adequate home financing system through insurance of mortgage loans, and to stabilize the mortgage market.

10. **United States Department of Housing and Urban Development**—also known as **HUD**, a Cabinet department in the Executive branch of the United States federal government. Although its beginnings were in the House and Home Financing Agency, it was founded as a Cabinet department in 1965, as part of the "Great Society" program of President Lyndon Johnson, to develop and execute policies on housing and metropolises.

Part I   Comprehension of the Text

1. Why did the author say that he knew very well why the Americans don't like their cities?

2. What do the Americans think of their cities?

3. For what reasons did the people of the other countries move to the United States according to the passage?

4. Why did the author claim that largely unskilled workers replacing the middle income New Yorkers who fled the city represented a further cost rather than an economic asset in many instances?

5. How did the American anti-urban attitude prevent the development of the modern city?

Part II   Vocabulary

A. Choose the one from the four choices that best explains the underlined word or phrase.

1. It seems <u>absurd</u> to seek a reduction in within-profession inequality at the cost of living standards for the actual poor.

   A. insensible   B. abnormal   C. ridiculous   D. unusual

2. Televisions play an <u>integral</u> part of our life these days as it has a powerful influence in developing value systems and shaping behaviour of individuals.

   A. essential   B. necessary   C. intellectual   D. intelligent

3. We have the responsibility to assure that this legacy, with its broad <u>dispersion</u> of land ownership, is passed on to our children and grandchildren.

   A. proportion   B. diversion   C. separation   D. distribution

4. We are doomed to repeat the failed patterns of life if we do not discover the truths of <u>authentic</u> manhood.

   A. authoritative   B. authorized   C. genuine   D. artificial

5. China has <u>accelerated</u> steps to diversify its foreign reserves basket by doubling South Korean debt holdings.

   A. quickened   B. transformed   C. adjusted   D. constrained

6. There are a lot of things <u>impertinent</u> to the case about her which would have been better left unrevealed.

   A. imperative   B. irrelevant   C. important   D. implicit

7. Many people are still stuck with the <u>assumption</u> that targeting a big market equals to big sales, which is far from the truth.

   A. prospective   B. expectation   C. anticipation   D. supposition

8. The U. S. Congress, the <u>legislative</u> branch of the federal government, consists of two houses: the Senate and the House of Representatives.

   A. law-making   B. general   C. lawful   D. legitimate

9. Both temples were <u>laid out</u> by men who were aware of identical methods at somewhat the same time period.

    A. designated   B. investigated   C. designed   D. constructed

10. This is a subject that, <u>on the face of it</u>, seems very simple but it is often misinterpreted so it demands further clarification.

    A. actually   B. apparently   C. definitely   D. undoubtedly

B. Choose the one from the four choices that best completes the sentence.

1. We are constantly being inundated with reports on how technology is making the world a cold, _____ place.

    A. desolate   B. isolate   C. enjoyable   D. obsolete

2. A record number of people flocked to the British Museum last year to see China's famous Terracotta Army on display.

    A. fled   B. popped   C. flocked   D. blocked

3. In today's technological age, dreaming of an old typewriter, for instance, might highlight an _____ to new technology.

    A. antiquity   B. antipathy   C. antibody   D. empathy

4. Hundreds of thousands of _____ have returned home from the battlefield with serious and life-altering injuries.

    A. veterans   B. veterinarians   C. vegetarians   D. adventurers

5. The human child goes through a long period of growth before he can _____ for himself in any meaningful way.

    A. rend   B. fend   C. lend   D. tend

6. A young and ambitious lawyer finds himself in a terrible _____ when he realizes his new boss and patron is actually the devil.

    A. predicament   B. prerequisite   C. preoccupation   D. preposition

7. With the number of divorces in the U. S. , _____ against single parents in the workplace is a serious issue to contend with.

    A. dissatisfaction   B. discrimination   C. disappointment   D. disintegration

8. At the onset, the only way for a house to generate cash is by renting it to other people or taking out a _____ on it.

    A. mortality   B. sabotage   C. litigation   D. mortgage

9. Governments _____ success with an educated workforce that will contribute to economic growth and promote good citizenship.

    A. attribute   B. augment   C. equate   D. transcend

10. Built in 1937, this particular brick house has undergone major _____ to create a romantic and functional housing.

    A. renovation   B. innovation   C. motivation   D. salvation

C. Complete each sentence with the proper form of the word given in the parenthesis.

1. Social workers are sensitive to cultural and ethnic diversity and strive to end poverty, discrimination, oppression, and other forms of social _____. (just)

2. His influence on the business reflects the honesty and hard work that he has _____ throughout his working life. (symbol)

3. Sleep experts believe that sleep _____ and inadequate sleep is becoming frightfully common and it can be bad for health in more ways than one. (deprive)

4. Children who are praised and encouraged develop a sense of competence, while those who are discouraged are left with a sense of _____. (inferior)

5. The purpose of _____ housing is to provide affordable housing for people who don't have a lot of money. (subsidy)

6. From the start, _____ meant the transformation of countries' populations from being predominantly rural to being predominantly urban. (industry)

7. The ceiling height creates a sense of _____ and does not at any time give the feeling that one is in an underground car park. (space)

8. Climate change will directly affect future food _____ and compound the difficulties of feeding the world's rapidly growing population. (avail)

9. By _____ Rousseau meant that man had the ability to improve on the qualities that he possessed and to pass these improvements on as part of the human heritage. (perfect)

10. Only those who spread treachery, fire, and death out of hatred for the prosperity of others are _____ of pity. (deserve)

Part III Cloze

Directions: There are totally 15 blanks in the following passage. Choose the best one to fill in each blank.

There are roughly three New Yorks. There is, first, the New York of the man or woman who was born here, who takes the city for __1__ and accepts its size and its turbulence __2__ natural and inevitable. Second, there is the New York of the commuter—the city that is __3__ by locusts each day and spat out each night. Third, there is the New York of the person who was born somewhere else and came to New York in __4__ of something. Of these three trembling cities the greatest is the last— the city of final __5__, the city that is a goal. It is this third city that __6__ for New York's high-strung disposition, its poetical deportment, its __7__ to the arts, and its incomparable achievements. __8__ give the city its tidal restlessness, natives give it solidarity and continuity, but the settlers give it __9__. And whether it is a farmer arriving from Italy to __10__ a small grocery store in a slum, or a young girl arriving from a small town in Mississippi to escape the __11__ of being observed by her neighbors, or a boy arriving from the Corn Belt with a __12__ in his suitcase and a pain in his heart, it makes no __13__: each embraces New York with the intense __14__ of first love, each absorbs New York with the fresh eyes of an adventurer, each __15__ heat and light to dwarf the Consolidated Edison Company.

1. A. graded   B. granted   C. graced   D. grated
2. A. as   B. for   C. by   D. with
3. A. crowded   B. congested   C. damaged   D. devoured
4. A. response   B. charge   C. quest   D. accord
5. A. destruction   B. destination   C. destitution   D. destiny
6. A. accounts   B. appeals   C. prepares   D. ascends
7. A. appreciation   B. attraction   C. contribution   D. dedication
8. A. Travelers   B. Commuters   C. Immigrants   D. Migrants
9. A. passion   B. anguish   C. hatred   D. despair
10. A. turn up   B. make up   C. set up   D. take up
11. A. contempt   B. depression   C. discomfort   D. indignity
12. A. transcript   B. manuscript   C. duplicate   D. stationery
13. A. difference   B. distinction   C. discrepancy   D. discrimination
14. A. anticipation   B. expectation   C. excitement   D. compassion
15. A. assimilates   B. illuminates   C. integrates   D. generates

Part IV   Writing

Directions：Develop each of the following topics into an essay of about 200 words.

1. Where to live—in the city or in the countryside?
2. Traffic Congestion in the City
3. Urban Life and Rural Life

Section B Extensive Reading and Translation

The Future of Urban Development

By Judith Rodin

[1] There is a potential roadmap that would enable cities to be engines of growth, while at the same time fortifying them to be more resilient. (1) Our experience of no more than 50 years of work on urbanization leads us to focus on building and strengthening the *infrastructures* that help communities bounce back from shocks like the "Great Recession", while more effectively leveraging the many opportunities of globalization.

[2] In cities, three critical infrastructures are required to achieve the twin goals of building resilience and leveraging more equitable economic growth. (2) First, the most successful cities have the *physical* infrastructure required to withstand and deflect disruptive shocks, including those related to global warming, which is the foremost *physical* manifestation of globalization.

[3] Sea levels are likely to rise three feet by the year 2100. That would put thousands of square miles of U.S. coastline, and many of its largest coastal cities, under water. And it would displace tens of millions of people in Asia, where huge cities on coasts and river deltas are at risk of becoming uninhabitable.

[4] (3) To help cities build the physical infrastructure they need to thrive during this time of unpredictable and unprecedented change, the Rockefeller Foundation formed the Asian Cities Climate Change Resilience Network (ACCCRN), which enables cities to grow in a manner that acknowledges and prepares for the possible ravages of a more unpredictable climate. This network helps some 70 million people in ten Asian cities develop and identify best practices for climate-resilient growth and develops effective, agile ways to implement those practices. These are also being scaled and transferred worldwide. Think of what a difference this would have made if it had been done in New Orleans or Port Au Prince.

[5] Likewise, designing more compact cities makes those cities more physically resilient by

reducing congestion and driving times, reducing dependence on fossil fuels and reducing CO_2. While a new type of physical infrastructure is paramount in an age of global climate change, *economic* infrastructure is equally critical in this era of globalization.

[6] Building economic resilience means that cities must have economies that are *diverse* enough to withstand financial shocks and *innovative* enough to seize the opportunities presented by globalization and even by challenges like climate change. (4) Particularly in Europe and the United States, given high unemployment, slow-going economic recovery and increased vulnerability to climate change, a new growth model based on a low-carbon economy would generate green jobs, diversify urban economies and promote greater prosperity.

[7] As we see from the Global Monitor report, fast-growing, successful cities around the world are those that capitalize most effectively on the hand that globalization has dealt. We have not been doing this lately in the United States—but we could. The Economic Policy Institute and the Center for American Progress estimate that an annual investment of $ 150 billion in clean energy in the United States would lead to a 1% drop in the unemployment rate. That, in turn, would lead to a rise in average earnings of about 2%, while building a more energy-sustainable infrastructure and creating 1.7 million jobs—half of which would be accessible to Americans with a high school degree or less.

[8] (5) In other words, green jobs are one area where it may be possible to promote economic resilience for the working poor and put the U.S. economy on a more resilient, sustainable path to growth, without the episodes of boom and bust that have characterized recent business cycles. And if that occurs, is it hard to imagine a transformation to more sustainable American cities—cities with greater density, increased walkability and energy efficient rapid transit and temperature control? This is by no means a radical suggestion, as it is sometimes considered domestically. Green cities are now being designed from the ground up in China, the Middle East and elsewhere, implementing this vision and at the same time creating thousands of new jobs in new green sectors—from housing to transportation to conservation. We in the United States are disturbingly behind the global curve in building for this kind of sustainable economic resilience.

[9] In addition to physical and economic resilience, we need a resilient *social* infrastructure as well, one that enriches our cities, makes them truly livable and underpins many of the efforts and opportunities I've described above. The Rockefeller Foundation promotes interventions that build a stronger community and civic infrastructure. For example, Americans' sense of volunteerism and community responsibility can be coordinated and leveraged for greater impact. One effort is Cities of Service—a coalition of U.S. mayors, each with an effective plan to coordinate citywide service strategies, engage diverse, local citizens as partners with cities and focus volunteer efforts on city priorities and meaningful outcomes. These cities have a point person with the executive power and the full-time responsibility to foster volunteerism.

[10] Let me give you a very practical example. In spring 2010, when tremendous flooding in Nashville, Tennessee, killed nearly three dozen people, the city's Chief Service Officer used her award-winning Cities of Service plan to quickly activate 17,000 local residents to assist in and manage aspects of the relief and clean-up effort. Nashville's mayor, Karl Dean, attributed a swift response and recovery not to the Federal Emergency Management Agency (FEMA), not to state authorities or

to his local officials, but to the volunteerism plan the city had developed as part of its application to Cities of Service. It allowed the people of Nashville to organize and activate an unprecedented volunteer effort.

[11] In conclusion, no recent development is more pressing—or promising—than accelerating urbanization the world over. Greater attention needs to be paid to the transformative impact of global urbanization and its profound challenges and opportunities. With clear and compelling evidence that this future will be distinctly and powerfully urban, we can't go back. We must build new and more resilient physical, economic and social infrastructures for the 21st century, as we come out of the Great Recession.

Part A Translate English into Chinese

I. Translate the underlined sentences in the above text into Chinese.

II. Translate paragraphs 9 and 11 in the above text into Chinese.

Part B Translate Chinese into English

I. Translate the following sentences into English with the words or phrases in the passage in Section B.

1. 中国政府在宣布实行和平统一的方针时,是基于一个前提,即世界上只有一个中国,台湾是中国的一部分。

2. 在应对国际金融危机的困难情况下,我们更加注重保障和改善民生,切实解决人民群众最关心、最直接、最现实的利益问题。

3. 当约翰从癌症中意外地康复时,他的医生把此归功于他坚强的毅力和对未来的信念。

4. 为了缓解奥运期间的交通拥堵状况,北京在那期间采取了单双号限行措施。

5. 市政府在公共服务上有这样庞大的投资,使市民人人都能享受既方便又能负担得起的优质健康医疗服务。

II. Translate the following paragraph into English.

    如果你对农村宁静生活的点滴乐趣能忍痛割爱的话,那么你就会发现城市可以为你提供生活中所必需的一切最好的东西。你不必跑好几英里路去看朋友;他们就住在附近,随时都可以谈天或晚间聚会。再说城市也不是没有优美的时刻。在寒冷潮湿的冬夜,令人感到舒适的是广告牌发出的暖光。每到周末,成千上万个每日来城里上班的人返回乡间的家中,市内大街上人迹稀少,此时没有什么能比这宁静的气氛更令人难忘了。为什么城市居民对这一切都很欣赏,却固执地装作宁愿住在乡村,这一直使我百思不得其解。